Assassins Of The Dead 5
Duke's Courier

Assassins Of The Dead 5 Duke's Courier

Avril Sabine

Cracked Acorn Productions
Australia

Assassins Of The Dead 5: Duke's Courier

Published by

Cracked Acorn Productions

PO Box 1365

Gympie, Queensland 4570

Australia

978-1-925941-43-2 (EPUB)

978-1-925941-44-9 (Print)

Genre: Young Adult Fantasy/Paranormal

Cover design by Caitlyn Petersen

For AKB. Because.

**Some heroes work in the shadows,
only their deeds remembered.**

Meikah had thought their tasks in Port Mayren were done. After being summoned to the headquarters of the Assassins Of The Dead, she soon found she was wrong. This time, things were personal. One of her family was in danger and she didn't know if she had the skills to rescue them as well as prevent the deaths of over a hundred innocent people.

*

This story was written by an Australian author using Australian spelling.

Name Pronunciation

Like many names there is more than one way to pronounce the following ones. These are the pronunciations used in this story.

Amiel (ah-meel)
Branok (bran-ock)
Breena (bree-nah)
Daveth (dav-eth)
Ena (en-ah)
Ervass (er-vas)
Galzeren (gal-zair-en)
Garven (garven)
Hincke (hink)
Isha (ee-sha)
Kellan (kell-en)
Letha (lee-thah)
Livia (liv-ee-ah)
Maksim (mack-sim)
Marta (mar-ta)
Meikah (mee-cah)

Mezeth (mez-eth)

Naya (neigh-ah)

Sirena (sigh-ren-ah)

Timell (tim-ill)

Tolmerr (toll-mer)

Chapter One

Meikah stood beside Kellan on the deck of the old timber sailing boat, her gaze fixed on the dock ahead of them, the weathered timber looking like the next storm might pull it apart. The last light of the day filled the sky with vibrant colours, the ocean tinged with them. Brushing the strands of her rich brown hair back from her face, that had come out of the plait hanging down her back, she tried to focus on their plans to return home soon, rather than think about the depressing day they'd had.

It had started with a visit to the school for wayward students, their cover story for being in Port Mayren. She pitied anyone who was sent there, its atmosphere made her think of a prison. The students had kept their heads lowered, but she'd noticed more than a handful of them sending daggered looks towards the teachers. And not a single one of the teachers had smiled. They'd had hard expressions and in one case pursed lips and a deep frown. Meikah had been glad to leave and even more glad the school wasn't in her future. At least she'd been glad until they'd reached Durnning Island, where they'd paid

Shorty, the grizzled old man who owned the boat they were on, to take them.

Meikah had hated telling Daveth and Marta they'd been random victims caught up in a plot against Timell, a previous King, and their deaths hadn't been personal. Nor could she help them return to their home with the dragons, even though Mezeth, one of the ancestor dragons, would have welcomed the two of them home. Or at least she would have welcomed them home if she had the ability to see and talk to the spirits.

Meikah sighed. Her plan to think of going home wasn't working. She'd only been gone from Dreyton for three days. Obviously not long enough to have missed it and have it on her mind.

Kellan glanced at Meikah before returning his attention to the dock they'd nearly reached. His black hair was tied at the nape of his neck, many of the strands having escaped to blow about his face in the cool breeze. "We should do something more interesting tonight. See some of the sights around the city or something before it's time to return home."

"Your 'something more interesting' usually gets us in trouble and I don't think the King will be as lenient as the Duke." Meikah's gaze momentarily collided with Kellan's and she couldn't miss seeing the mischief in his brown eyes.

Kellan chuckled. "I bet he'd be lenient if you're involved. Especially since you saved his city from being destroyed by a dragon yesterday."

"No, I saved a dragon from being destroyed by him and his city," Meikah corrected. "She was the one held prisoner."

"She would have figured out a way to escape and then destroyed the city and all the countryside for miles around," Kellan said. "If not further."

Meikah's gaze was drawn to the back of her right hand where the silhouette of a dragon in flight sometimes appeared. She'd never asked to be dragon touched, but during the past few days she'd been glad for Letha's so-called gift. With it she'd been able to save the life of an ancestor dragon and possibly the lives of Port Mayren if Kellan was right and Mezeth had escaped. She met Kellan's gaze, drawing in a breath at the intensity of the look he gave her. She was still uncertain what she should do about his interest in her. It wasn't like she was uninterested, but the two of them had to work together and if things didn't work out between them, how would they manage to do that? She again looked at the dock, determined not to focus on such thoughts. Not after the day she'd already had. They slowed as they approached the dock and she was surprised to see a figure dressed in dark clothes, the hood of a jacket pulled up to shadow his face. But she didn't need to see his face to know who it was.

She turned to Kellan. "Did you ask Shade to meet us here?"

Kellan shook his head. "Maybe he has something interesting for us to do." He strode towards the front of the boat and tossed a rope to Shade who caught it and tied it off.

Before clambering out of the boat, Meikah thanked Shorty, who nodded in answer, arms crossed as he watched them leave.

"Do you finally have a reply to take back to the Duke?" Kellan asked Shade as they strode towards the horses grazing under a tree well back from the beach.

"In a manner of speaking." Shade gathered up the reins of his horse.

"What sort of manner?" Meikah swung into the saddle, turning her horse to face Port Mayren. It wasn't that far along the coast from them. "Or do you mean we now have something else we need to wait for before we can go home?"

"Tolmerr has asked to see us," Shade said.

"Who?" Meikah glanced at Shade. What little she could see of his face, in the shadows created by his hood, was unreadable.

"The Commander," Shade said.

Meikah stared at him for a moment. The leader of the entire Assassins Of The Dead faction wanted to see them? Her included? "All of us?"

"He mentioned the two of you by name," Shade said.

"Did he say what it's about?" Kellan asked.

"Only that he had the answer the Duke sought and to bring the two of you to headquarters." Shade glanced at each of them. "He isn't like Danton. He doesn't sit down with his people for meals and he certainly doesn't talk to them like they're part of his family."

"What is he like?" Meikah couldn't help thinking of the teachers at the school for wayward students. Was he like them?

"He sticks to the rules, is fair, but tends to be rather distant with people," Shade said. "That is, he is fair unless you've done something wrong and then I hear he can be quite harsh."

Meikah thought about everything they'd done since arriving. Had they done anything wrong? She supposed she'd soon find out. "Should we call in and let Grandmother Isha know where we're going?"

"I stopped in there looking for you," Shade said. "She directed me to Shorty's."

Meikah hadn't liked to involve her grandmother in Assassins Of The Dead business, but she hadn't wanted to return to the island without letting someone know where they were going. Not after the last time they'd been out there.

Kellan spoke, interrupting Meikah's thoughts. "I wonder what the letter the Duke sent to Tolmerr said. A pity we couldn't have read it before we handed it over."

"I doubt we'll find out exactly what it said, but if we're given a verbal answer to pass along, at least it'll give us an idea of what the question might have been." Shade nudged his horse to pick up speed. "It took you longer to return from the island than I expected. The Commander's been waiting a few hours now. Even though he didn't say it was important, I've been told he doesn't like to be kept waiting."

Meikah nudged her horse to match the pace of Shade's mount, Kellan also doing the same. They remained quiet as they headed towards Cryptic Ramblings. Obscure Texts And Scrolls, the bookshop the Assassins Of The Dead used for their headquarters in Port Mayren. They left their horses at the stable used by the local Assassins Of The Dead and headed inside.

She stopped in the doorway of the bookshop while her eyes grew accustomed to the shadowy interior. It didn't take long since there'd been very little light outside. She scanned the area. It was a larger bookshop than Fable. Tomes Of The Arcane. And a much older building.

"This way." Shade led the way to behind the counter where they slipped through a curtained doorway, heading straight up a set of stairs from the hallway behind the curtain. He stopped at one of the doors along the upstairs hallway that was guarded by a young man.

"He's waiting for you." The young man stepped to the side, nodding towards the door.

Shade knocked sharply.

There was silence for a moment and then a voice called out, "Enter."

Shade swung the door open and ushered them in, closing it once they were inside. "Commander Tolmerr, we're reporting as requested."

Chapter Two

Meikah stared at the slim man who rose from where he sat behind a dark timber desk, taller than Kellan. When Kellan said nothing, meeting the Commander's gaze, she wondered if that was proper etiquette or Kellan's typical disregard for how things were done.

"I received reports on what you did to keep Port Mayren safe," Tolmerr said. "You all acquitted yourself admirably."

"We did what any Assassin Of The Dead would have done," Kellan said.

Tolmerr inclined his head. "Shall we get straight to the point?" He gestured towards the four chairs in front of his desk, his gaze remaining on Meikah. He waited until the three of them were seated before he also sat down. "One of the Duke's agents is missing."

Meikah wished he'd look at either of the other two and then wondered if she'd somehow missed something. Had she offended him somehow?

"Do we know the agent?" Kellan asked.

Tolmerr barely glanced at Kellan before returning his attention to Meikah. "It would seem that the agent has been captured by the people he was investigating." He took an envelope from a drawer of his desk, holding it out to Meikah. "I thought you might be interested in this job since we can't very well leave him in the predicament he's currently in. The assassin who tracked him down said that at a glance it seems to be a simple matter to deal with. He was only tasked with finding the whereabouts of the agent, not bringing him home."

Meikah frowned at the envelope, wondering if she should hand it to Kellan since he was the one who tended to be in charge of their group.

"Thanks." Kellan started to rise. "We'll go over the details and see what we can do about rescuing the Duke's agent."

"Sit down, Kellan. I didn't give the job to you because you're from Dreyton." Tolmerr turned to Meikah. "You might wish to open the envelope before you leave my office."

"Me?" Meikah felt her cheeks heat from actually speaking the question aloud instead of opening the envelope like Tolmerr had suggested.

Tolmerr nodded. "Go ahead. Open it." He remained silent as she drew the folded pieces of paper from the envelope, not speaking until she'd taken all of them out. "The agent appeared to be in reasonable health, the last time someone saw him, according to the assassin who tracked him down."

All words Meikah might have spoken vanished when she opened the first piece of paper to read over the opening paragraph of the report. She pressed a finger against the paper, pointing to the name as she met Tolmerr's gaze. "Maksim. As in my grandfather?" She held her breath as she waited for him to say no. It took her a moment to realise he'd given a single nod and she released her breath in a rush. "But he no longer does this kind of work. He's retired from active missions. Now he deals with diplomatic ones." Or at least that's what everyone had been told. "He's the Duke's courier."

"Was this a diplomatic mission?" Shade asked.

"It would appear not," Tolmerr said. "I'm afraid your grandfather is still an active agent of the Duke and not one who deals with diplomatic incidences."

Meikah slowly shook her head. "It can't be Grandfather Maksim. He was…" Her voice trailed off as she thought of how long he'd been gone. "What do I tell Grandmother Isha?" Did her grandmother know her husband still went on active missions? Or did she believe the same story everyone else believed? That he was the Duke's courier.

"I suggest you read the report first." Tolmerr glanced at the door. "You may take it with you. I had that copy made for you."

Meikah rose from the chair, stunned by the news. It didn't seem possible. Surely her grandfather wasn't doing active missions. Not these days. Although he always seemed younger than Grandfather Harlen, even though they were of a similar age, so it wouldn't be impossible for him to go on active missions.

Kellan guided Meikah through the doorway. "I know somewhere quiet where we can read the report."

She nodded, her thoughts a jumble as she followed Kellan along the hallway.

"We will get him back for you," Kellan assured her.

"Tolmerr said he was in reasonable health," Shade pointed out.

She nodded, her gaze drawn back to the pieces of paper she held, only one of them unfolded. What was she going to tell Grandmother Isha? She couldn't stop worrying about that.

Kellan stepped back to let Meikah enter a small sitting room that was currently unoccupied. There was a group of four armchairs clustered around a fireplace and tall bookcases on the far wall with a narrow window set in the middle of the wall, a shorter bookcase beneath it.

Dropping onto one of the chairs, she stared at the pieces of paper a moment longer before she could bring herself to start reading them. The words made no sense, the images in her mind of her grandfather in the way of them.

Kellan took the papers from her when she looked up. "Let me see what they say so we can start making plans."

She started to protest, the words remaining unspoken. It wasn't like she could make sense of anything. All she could think about was the possibility of losing Maksim and having to tell Isha.

Kellan looked up from the pieces of paper. "The first thing we need to do is find out more about this village."

"Where is it?" Shade asked.

Kellan handed him one of the pieces of paper.

Shade looked it over before giving a single nod and handing it back to Kellan. "Night is the perfect time to learn more about an area. I'll meet you at your uncle Garven's house as soon as I learn anything."

Meikah watched Shade stride from the room. It wasn't until he was out of sight that she realised she hadn't thanked him. She half rose, then sat down again. He was probably out of the bookshop by now.

"What's wrong?" Kellan asked. "Other than the obvious."

"I didn't thank him."

Kellan took hold of her hand. "He knows. You don't need to say anything." Rising to his feet, he looked down at her. "Did you want to tell Isha now or wait until Shade returns with some news?"

"I'm not sure how to tell her."

"I'll help you." He drew her to her feet, guiding her from the bookshop and to the stable where they'd left the horses.

Meikah had no idea how they reached Garven's house. The ride was a blur of unrelated images and she was thankful Kellan had been with her. Logically she knew her grandfather had put himself in danger her entire life, but being faced with the reality that he might die was far different from knowing it could happen. It also didn't help that she'd thought him safe these days. Or at least far safer than when she'd known he was being sent on a mission.

She glanced over her shoulder, wondering how they'd gone from the front door to the kitchen where Isha talked to Garven's housekeeper. Amongst the fragments of her evening were memories of her grandfather. Unlike Harlen, Maksim had actually enjoyed spending time with her and her sister. Nor had he expected more from her or Ena than they were interested in achieving. He'd even encouraged them to follow their own interests rather than what was expected of them by family tradition.

Isha looked up from her discussion with the house-keeper, the smile of greeting fading. She hurried forward. "What happened, Meikie?" She wrapped her arms around her granddaughter. "Tell me what's wrong."

"Can we go to-" Meikah broke off as she realised she had no idea where they should go. This wasn't something she wanted to tell Isha in front of the housekeeper. The woman had more than enough to gossip about without giving her something that should be kept quiet.

"The study," Kellan said.

Meikah nodded, wanting to protest when Isha let her go. She followed Kellan to the study, frequently glancing over her shoulder to make sure Isha followed.

Chapter Three

Once they were in the study, and seated, Meikah couldn't bring herself to look in her grandmother's direction. Nor could she find the words to tell her Maksim was in serious trouble.

"Tell me what happened, Meikie."

"Did you want me to explain?" Kellan asked.

Meikah shook her head, drawing in a deep breath as she tried to find the words. "It's Grandfather Maksim."

Isha frowned. "What do you mean it's Maksim? What about Maksim?"

"He's been captured." Meikah gave all the pieces of paper to Isha. "He was on a mission for the Duke and it seems like the people he was investigating caught him."

Isha looked up from the piece of paper she was reading. "Why were you informed? Why didn't they come to me? Why did they send you to tell me?"

Kellan drew out the Assassins Of The Dead medallion that hung at his neck. "We weren't sent to inform you, we've been assigned the task of bringing him home." He slid the medallion back under his shirt. "No one said anything about keeping the information from you, and Meikah wanted to tell you."

Isha stared open-mouthed at Kellan for a moment, even after the medallion had been tucked away, before closing her mouth and turning to Meikah. "You as well, Meikie?"

Meikah drew her medallion out from beneath her shirt, answering with a nod since words seemed difficult to form.

Isha closed her eyes for nearly a minute, meeting Meikah's gaze when she opened them. "What needs to be done first? How can I help?"

At the strength she heard in her grandmother's voice, Meikah straightened her shoulders. Surely if her grandmother could keep herself from falling apart than she should be able to do no less. "Shade has gone to search the area and learn what he can about the village." She tucked the medallion out of sight again.

"All three of you work for the King?" Isha asked.

"In a manner of speaking," Kellan said.

"How would you put it then?" Isha asked.

"We work for the people of this country." Kellan grinned. "Which sometimes conflicts with what the King wants."

Isha studied Meikah for a moment before she nodded. "That Harlen always said Ena was the one who'd go places. But I knew you were destined for greatness. Just like my Maksim."

"Grandmother Isha-"

Isha interrupted Meikah. "I won't accept any modest protests." She looked between the two of them. "When is Shade due back?"

"We came here the moment he left," Kellan said. "I'd be surprised if he returns before dawn."

Isha met Kellan's gaze, her expression determined. "I expect to be involved in rescuing my husband."

"As long as it doesn't put him in more danger," Kellan said.

"That's fair." Isha rose to her feet. "I'll see that dinner is ready as soon as possible so we can have an early night." She strode from the study, leaving silence in her wake.

Kellan eventually grinned, turning to Meikah. "I've always liked Isha."

"Maybe we should have asked Tolmerr to send someone more experienced than us," Meikah said.

"He wouldn't have assigned us if the mission needed more experienced assassins. He's not the sort to do that. He's very much by the book and into following proper protocols."

"We need to get Maksim back for Grandmother Isha." Meikah didn't say she also needed her grandfather. But she did. He was one of her favourite people. Him and Isha. And she'd spent a lot of time with them over the years. Time that she'd enjoyed every minute of. Not like the time she'd spent with Harlen and Sirena. Both lots of her grandparents were completely different from each other.

"We will get him back," Kellan stated. "For both of you."

She met his gaze, seeing the promise within his eyes and a hint of the mist that meant his magic was ready to be used if he should need it. She didn't doubt him in the least. Not with how certain he sounded. "Thank you." The panic she'd initially felt receded. Isha's determination and Kellan's certainty made her feel that rescuing Maksim was possible. More than possible. That he'd be back with them in no time. "I'll help Isha and the housekeeper prepare dinner. I'm not sure how well I'll sleep, but an early night is probably a good plan." She wanted to go after Maksim the moment Shade returned with information about the village. The only reason she hadn't demanded to go after her grandfather immediately she'd discovered he'd been captured was that learning all they could about Maksim's situation made sense. It'd give them the best possible chance of freeing him.

Dinner was accompanied by grumbles from Garven about how early the meal had been served and Meikah escaped to her room the moment it was over. She'd expected to take forever to fall asleep, but a day out on the ocean had obviously helped and she was asleep within minutes.

Kellan woke her when the light was creeping into her room, the sun not yet risen. He silently beckoned her to follow and she walked lightly behind him, having gone to bed dressed in clothes ready to leave. He led her to the study where a single lamp was lit, Shade standing to the side of the window and Isha seated in one of the chairs.

"Is he well?" Meikah blurted out.

Shade gestured towards a seat, remaining silent.

Meikah hurriedly sat down. "Well?"

"The village has only been there for a few months according to farmers in the area. The walls went up one week, guards were manning them the following week," Shade said.

"What does that mean?" Meikah asked.

"Villages form for a reason," Kellan said.

"What was the reason this village formed?" Isha asked.

Shade shrugged. "They don't trade with the locals and they don't talk with them. They keep to themselves and supply wagons come in on a regular schedule twice a week. It was impossible to get past the walls that towered above all the features of the land, which also made it impossible to see past them. None of the local farmers could think of any natural resource that would be in that location or any other reason for the village to be there."

"What about Grandfather Maksim?" Meikah asked.

"Did you not hear the part where I said it's impossible to see past the walls?" Shade asked. "The only information I could gain was the same as the assassin who tracked him down. A farmer saw him being led into the village by armed guards."

"Yes, but–"

Kellan interrupted Meikah. "When is the next supply wagon due?"

"In two day's time," Shade said.

"We might be able to sneak onto the wagon and get past the walls that way," Kellan suggested.

"That's too many days away," Meikah protested.

"According to local farmers, the supply wagons are heavily guarded," Shade said. "It would be impossible to sneak on them while they're on the road. I don't know how well guarded the wagons will be while they're being loaded, but that might be the only way to sneak onto a supply wagon if we use that method of entering the village."

"What happens to the wagons after they reach the village?" Kellan asked.

"They enter the village full and leave empty the afternoon they arrive," Shade said.

"When do they return?" Isha asked.

Shade didn't answer immediately. "They come back in three days and then it's four days before the next lot arrives."

"A week," Meikah exclaimed. "You want my grandfather to wait a week to be rescued?"

"We can continue to try and find a way in there while Shade works on that angle," Kellan suggested.

"Such as what?" Meikah demanded.

Isha put a hand on Meikah's arm. "Meikie, Maksim has been in worse situations than this. I'm sure with your help, and that of your friends, he'll get through this as well."

Chapter Four

Meikah didn't want to think about the possibility of them not rescuing her grandfather. "When do we leave?"

After some discussion, and a few minor arguments, they settled on a cover story and Shade went to gather supplies, taking with him some of the money Danton had given Kellan for their stay in Port Mayren. Everything felt like it took too long to Meikah, and she wished she could remain as calm as Isha. How had she managed a lifetime of not knowing if her husband would come home? And not only manage, but remain calm in the face of it all.

As they gathered their gear and prepared for the mission, Meikah regularly checked Isha, wanting to make sure her grandmother was holding up. Each time she appeared calm and determined. Meikah was occasionally tempted to ask Isha how she really felt. To ask if she was as calm as she looked. But they didn't have time for such discussions. They needed to get ready.

They dressed in serviceable clothes, the material course and the colours faded, the boots they wore equally worn looking. Although Meikah had discovered upon exam-ination that the boots were in better condition than they appeared. They left their weapons behind as being armed wouldn't suit their cover and hid a couple of basic weapons in the actor's travelling wagon Shade had some-how procured. The wagon had a solid roof and contained costumes and props in case the villagers wanted proof they were the travelling actors they claimed to be.

By the time they left the city, Shade perched on the top of the wagon and Meikah sitting on the wagon seat next to Isha, Kellan on the other side of her grandmoth-er, Meikah couldn't help blurting out, "How do you manage?"

Isha turned to Meikah. "Manage what in particular, Meikie?"

"To stay so calm."

Isha smiled. "It wasn't always so easy. Then I realised this is who Maksim is. He's the one who faces trouble so others don't have to. The one who protects not only those he loves, but those in his country because he can't do other than protect. If he was any other way, he wouldn't be the Maksim I love. So I learned to accept and be grateful for every day I'm granted to have him in my life. There have been so many days, far more than I expected, that I continue to hope there'll be many more to come."

Meikah took hold of Isha's hand, holding it tight. "W-e'll make sure he gets through this trouble so he can keep protecting all of us."

Isha smiled again. "I have a feeling you're right there with him, protecting all of us from the trouble that comes our way. And stopping that trouble from ever reaching us."

Meikah thought of all she'd faced since discovering her abilities and being introduced to the Assassins Of The Dead. She returned Isha's smile. "Someone has to do it."

Isha laughed softly. "You're so like him. So very much like him." She tightened her grip on Meikah's hand. "I've lost count of the times he's said those exact words to me about the work he does."

"He has?" Meikah asked.

Isha nodded. "He certainly has."

For some reason, hearing that made Meikah feel less worried. It made no sense it had helped, but it had anyway. Keeping hold of her grandmother's hand, she fell silent, regularly scanning the forest they travelled through. The day remained quiet and nearly two hours into their journey, they pulled up.

Shade jumped down off the roof of the wagon where he'd been perched on top of it the entire time. He walked along the edge of the narrow dirt road that meandered through the trees, picking up a rock that filled his hand. Returning to the wagon, he smashed the rock against the wheel, examining his work. "It looks natural." He propped the wagon up with some rocks and logs before removing the wheel with the help of the handful of tools stored in the wagon.

Kellan turned to Meikah. "Ready to walk to the village with me? It should only be ten minutes from here." He glanced at Shade, who'd rolled the wheel over to him, and took the damaged wheel. "Thanks."

"Do you think they'll let us in to have it repaired?" Meikah asked.

Kellan grinned at her. "I guess we're about to find out."

Meikah turned to Isha who was sitting under a tree at the side of the road, Shade having given her a waterskin. "We'll be back as soon as possible."

"Take your time," Isha said. "These things can't be rushed."

The words rang in Meikah's mind as they strode in the direction of the village, Kellan rolling the wheel alongside him. Each time it reached the damaged section, he needed to use more force, causing an odd rhythm. Her gaze remained on the wheel while she thought over Isha's words. She'd been trying to rush the rescue. Her grandmother was right. A rescue shouldn't be rushed. Not if she wanted the rescue to work.

The last of her urgency faded and she focused on what they needed to do. The first was to get past the walls of the village so they could learn what was beyond them. Next was to figure out what defences they had and last was to discover where they were keeping Maksim so they could get him out of there. Hopefully, all that could be done while the wagon wheel was being repaired.

They saw the wall well before they reached it. Tall slabs of timber with pointed ends jutted up into the sky making a solid barricade that was interrupted by a double gate, the dirt road they followed ending at it. There was a large clearing in front of the wall and to either side as far as Meikah could see, the forest having been cut down to leave stumps to dot the clearing.

"Don't come any closer," a voice called out.

Meikah tried to spot where the voice came from. She didn't see the man until he stepped out of cover from behind a tree that edged the clearing. She stopped beside Kellan in the middle of the road, her gaze momentarily resting on the crossbow pointed at them.

"Our wheel needs repairing. We came down hard on a rock a bit up the road that way." Kellan glanced over his shoulder. "Less than ten minutes."

"We can't help you," the man said.

Kellan smiled, keeping his tone light and friendly. "Surely your wheelwright can do with a bit of extra coin."

"We don't have a wheelwright," the man said. "You'll have to take it to Port Mayren."

"Really? All that way?" Kellan ran the back of his arm across his forehead. "That's where we came from this morning. I doubt they'd welcome us back there." He glanced at Meikah, giving her a pointed glare.

If she hadn't been part of the planning, she would have believed him angry with her. "How was I supposed to know the woman was a spirit? It's only polite to apologise when you get in someone's way. She didn't look the way a spirit normally looks. I could have sworn she was living. They should have believed me when I said I wasn't a necromancer. I see the dead, not wield magic."

"You're a necromancer?" the man asked.

Chapter Five

Meikah let out a heavy sigh. "Why does everyone automatically think that? No, I'm not a necromancer. I've never been able to do magic, and no one in my family has been able to do it." She sighed yet again. "I just have an unfortunate ability to see the dead. My grandmother has the same ability. Oh, not the one who travels with us. The other one. The one on my father's side." Meikah was tempted to grin at the thought of Sirena being able to see the dead. The urge faded nearly as quickly as it had begun. Her gaze again drawn to the crossbow. Had he lowered it slightly?

"I can't help either of you. Necromancer or not," the man said. "You'll have to return to Port Mayren."

"Now?" Meikah asked. "We've just dragged the wheel all this way-"

The man interrupted her. "Ten minutes isn't far."

"It'll be twenty by the time we return to the wagon and hours more before we reach Port Mayren. There's no way we can get back to our wagon from Port Mayren before dark and we can't leave my grandmother and brother there on their own all night. Who knows what roams the forest," Meikah protested.

"Would you have a wagon wheel we can borrow?" Kellan asked. "And the directions to a place other than Port Mayren, since I doubt they'd let us back in the city after all the drama of chasing us out. And it was such a great play we put on for them last night too."

"You're actors?" the man asked.

Meikah nodded. "I was born and raised on the road. My family have been actors for generations." She looked suitably mournful. "If only they hadn't thought bringing culture to the Arcton Mountains was a good idea. Only a few of us managed to escape that lawless area with our lives."

"That explains it," the man said.

Meikah frowned. "Explains what?"

"All the drama about a ten-minute walk."

"That wasn't drama," Meikah protested. "Do you have something against actors?" She was beginning to wonder if they should have chosen a different cover story.

The man shook his head. "I was training to be an actor. A long time ago." His gaze became distant.

Meikah took a step towards him. "It's never too late."

The man shook his head, his gaze snapping back into focus. "That was another lifetime. Now you both need to move on."

"If you could help us out with the wheel, we could stay the night and perform for the village. We could even give you a few lessons in being an actor. Maybe let you play one of the parts we had to remove from the play when we lost so many during that terrible journey to the Arcton Mountains." Meikah had no idea how they'd manage to follow through on her offers, but she desperately needed to enter the village. They could figure the rest out later.

The man didn't speak immediately. "I'm afraid not." He glanced at the gates before returning his attention to them. "Now you both really need to move along. Some of the other guards aren't as friendly as I am."

When he hadn't immediately answered her, Meikah had started to hope he'd changed his mind. She had a feeling he'd been extremely tempted. Maybe they could convince him yet. "Do you want me to beg? Because I can if you want. I don't want to die out there in the forest because our wheel was broken." She took another small step towards him. "Please. We really need your help."

Another man strode towards them, coming out of the forest, this one with a sword at his side and a bow at his back. "What's going on here?"

The first man came to attention. "They've got a broken wheel, sir."

"Just the two of them?" the second man asked.

"At least four of them. Two in a wagon ten minutes back up the road."

"Four of them." The second man looked them up and down. "Any sorcerers amongst you? We're in need of the services of a sorcerer."

Meikah shook her head, once again wishing they'd come up with a different cover story.

"How many of you are there?" The man looked between the two of them.

"Four," Kellan said.

The man studied them a moment longer before he smiled. "How can we help you?"

Meikah forced herself not to retreat from his smile. If he was trying to set them at ease by making them think he was friendly, he was a long way off his goal. "Our wheel needs fixing." She glanced at the wheel Kellan rested his hand against.

"We can't go to Port Mayren, even if it was closer," Kellan said. "They ran us out of there this morning."

"The people there thought they were necromancers," the first man said. "Apparently they're not."

"But you can see the dead," the second man said.

Meikah nodded. "That doesn't make me able to do magic though."

The man slowly nodded. "I know. I know very well that the two can be separate." He pointed at the ground. "Wait here." Spinning on his heel, he strode to the gate, calling out for it to be opened.

Meikah caught a glimpse of the village before the gate was closed. A mixture of single and two-storey buildings. Not enough details to have a clear idea of what was behind the walls. They needed to see more than that if they were to figure out how to rescue Maksim. She turned to the man with the crossbow. "I'm sorry we've been such a bother." She smiled at him, certain she did a better job at being friendly than the other man had done.

The man with the crossbow glanced at the gate before lowering his voice. "You should go. The two of you. It's not safe around here. Collect your family and leave. Forget about your wagon and get to safety. You're too young to be wandering around the forest like this."

Meikah stared at him, her mouth partly open as she struggled to figure out how to react to his words. "I don't-"

"We can't leave our wagon behind," Kellan said. "It's our livelihood."

"It's a little hard to earn a living when you're dead," the man said.

Again Meikah had no idea what to say. Was he warning them about the area in general? Or about the village in particular.

"It sounds like you've already suffered more than enough misfortunes in your life," the man said. "So just go. While you still have the chance."

Meikah couldn't tell him she'd lost the chance the moment her grandfather had been captured. "There's nowhere we can go without our wagon. It's not only our livelihood, but also our means of travelling to places and it contains everything we own."

"Things can always be-" The man broke off with a glance towards the gate. He took a step back from them. "I'm sorry."

Meikah turned towards the gate that had opened enough to let several men exit the village, one of them carrying a wagon wheel. The man who'd been talking to them earlier led the group. He came towards them with the same smile, the one that made her uncomfortable. She instantly wished she could have taken the advice of the man with the crossbow. But she couldn't. Her grandfather was trapped inside their village.

"I'm Hincke." He smiled again. "These men have volunteered to help bring your wagon back so the wheel can be fixed."

"How can that be done if you don't have a wheelwright?" Kellan asked.

Hincke glanced at the man with the crossbow, his smile becoming more strained. "We'll send the wheel off to be repaired when the supply wagon arrives. In the meantime, you can stay with us while you wait. It's not safe out in the forest when you have such a small group of people in your travelling party."

One of the men came forward and took the wheel from Kellan, leaving it propped against the wall. Kellan gave him a nod in thanks before facing the way they'd come and heading along the road when Hincke asked him to show them the way.

Chapter Six

Meikah kept pace with Kellan, resisting the urge to regularly check those that followed them. That was after the first glance over her shoulder. The uncomfortable smile given to them by Hincke made her want to take cover and prepare to defend herself. She wanted to ask Kellan if they should have declined. Things weren't working out exactly like they'd planned and she had a feeling that wasn't good. Staying several days trapped behind the wall of the village wasn't even close to what they'd expected. A few hours at the most and then they'd planned to get out of there so they could work on a way to rescue Maksim. Now she had no idea what they'd do instead. Could they stage a rescue from inside the village? Or would they be watched too closely to plan things out between them? And what about Shade? He wouldn't know what they were going to do and couldn't help them with it.

When they arrived back at the wagon, it was to find Isha alone. Meikah was quite proud of her grandmother's performance when she complained about Shade taking off and heading back to the city, leaving her behind when anything could be lurking amongst the trees.

Isha finished with, "Our family has always been actors. How could he want to be anything other than an actor? I'm sure it was that pretty little barmaid turning his head. Nothing good will come of him settling down. He's not used to staying in one place for any length of time. He'll regret leaving us."

Hincke looked between the three of them. "He won't come back here looking for you?"

"He knows we don't stay anywhere for long and go where our feet take us," Isha said. "I told him if he walked off now, I'd wash my hands of him. After all I've done for him, he threw his clothes in a bag and walked off without a backwards glance."

"So he's not coming back and not expecting you to go after him?" Hincke asked.

Meikah stared at Hincke. It was beginning to sound very much like he wanted to make sure no one would come looking for them. Should they run before they ended up prisoners too? How were they meant to rescue Maksim if they ended up caught with him?

"Why would I want to go after him?" Isha demanded. "He was the one who left us. Good riddance. And after all I've done for him."

Meikah moved closer to Kellan, keeping her voice low while Hincke ordered his men to put the wheel on the wagon, telling them it was a close enough fit to travel so short a distance when they said it wasn't the correct size. "Should we be go–"

Kellan interrupted her, keeping his voice just as low. "We can't make Shade stay with us if he wants to do something as boring as live in a city." He gave her a warning look before glancing at Hincke.

Frustration arrowed through her. There had to be a way to discuss things with him. She was certain they were walking into a trap. Getting themselves caught would be a disaster.

Kellan smiled at her reassuringly, taking her hand and lightly squeezing before letting go.

She wasn't reassured in the least. Narrowing her eyes, she glanced at Hincke before returning her attention to Kellan.

Again he smiled. "I know you don't like to owe anyone, but maybe they'll let us put on a play in repayment for their help."

Hincke joined them. "No trouble at all. We're glad to help. You don't owe us a thing."

Meikah returned his insincere smile, absolutely certain that hers wasn't anywhere near as bad as his. For starters, she doubted her smile made him as uncomfortable as his smile made her. "That's so kind of you."

Hincke gestured towards the wagon that was starting to move off, two of his men on the seat with Isha seated between them. "We'll have you behind the walls and out of this forest in no time. It's not a good place to be. Hurry along now. You don't want to be left behind. There are all types of wildlife that come out once dark falls."

Meikah walked beside the wagon, Kellan next to her. She'd been so tempted to ask Hincke exactly where it wasn't a good place to be. The forest or the village. She had a feeling it was the village. A feeling that filled her with dread and made her want to decline his offer to remain in the village until their wheel was fixed. Silently following him felt wrong. She glanced at Kellan, who once again gave her a reassuring smile. He had to know they were walking into some kind of trap. He better have a good plan all figured out because they were taking Isha with them and she didn't want anything to happen to her grandmother.

As they approached the village, the gates swung open wide. The wagon was left beside a building that appeared to have no windows. They were led around to the other side of it, to the single opening in the entire building. A door. Meikah stood in front of it, clasping her hands together so she didn't reach for Kellan, who remained at her side. It took all her willpower not to run. Even though there was nowhere to run since the gate had been closed behind them when they'd entered the village.

Hincke started to unlock one of the several locks on the door as his men stood around, Isha being ushered towards them. "You'll find this interesting."

"Why's that?" Kellan asked.

Hincke only smiled as he continued to unlock the door. With a glance at his men, he swung it open.

Meikah turned to the sounds behind her. Weapons were drawn and pointed at them. "What is going on?" She tried to sound shocked, like she assumed the young, naive actor she was pretending to be would have reacted.

"Inside." Hincke snapped out the word, his tone sharp and demanding.

Isha moved closer to Meikah and Kellan. "It's dark in there."

"If I have to ask again, you will regret it," Hincke warned.

Meikah grabbed Isha's hand. Unlike herself, her grandmother could be killed permanently. "I'm sure this is just some sort of misunderstanding." She tugged Isha towards the open door. "They'll soon realise we don't belong in here. You'll see, Grandmother Isha. They'll be letting us out within an hour or so." She stopped a few feet inside the building, Kellan having followed her. She met Hincke's gaze. "If you're putting us in here because you think we're necromancers, you've got the wrong people."

Hincke chuckled. "Not at all. I don't doubt you're telling the truth about not being a necromancer. That doesn't mean you'll be let out of here in a few hours." He slammed the door shut.

Meikah drew in a shaky breath, unable to drag her gaze away from the door as she listened to it being locked. She wanted to ask Kellan what they were to do now, but she had no idea who was on the other side of the door and might hear her question. She turned her back on the door and the light coming in around it, needing to know where Hincke had put them. Using her ability to see in the dark, she breathed in sharply. The place was crowded. There had to be a hundred people in the building with them. Or possibly more.

"This can't be good," Kellan murmured.

Meikah slowly shook her head. "That's an understatement. Who are all these people?" Most of the people were ignoring them, many of them lying in cramped spots, some leaning against walls or other people.

"Meikah? Isha?" A man pushed his way through the crowd. "What are the two of you doing in here?" Maksim stopped in front of his wife, holding both her hands as he stared down at her. "Not the place I'd ever expect to find you, my love." His grey hair looked in need of a trim and as if it hadn't been brushed in weeks. His clothes were torn and hung loosely on him and he was barefoot.

"That is an interesting story," Isha said.

Kellan lay on the floor near the door, looking underneath it.

"They never stick around." Maksim kept hold of Isha's hands, his gaze on Kellan. "They dump the next person, or people, in here then leave again."

Kellan rose to his feet. "Why are we in here?"

Maksim shrugged. "I was caught before I could learn what's going on."

"Why did you think something was going on here?" Meikah asked. "What made you investigate this village?"

Maksim looked from Isha to Meikah. "How did the two of you end up following me in here? You did follow me, didn't you? Are you here to let me know rescue is on the way?"

Chapter Seven

Meikah drew out her Assassins Of The Dead amulet, holding it up for Maksim. "We were looking for you." She avoided answering his last question. Unless Shade decided to go for help, they were on their own. She had a feeling that would be a last resort for him.

Maksim took hold of the amulet, running his fingers over it before letting it go. "The three of you?" He glanced at each of them, his gaze coming to a rest on Isha.

Isha laughed softly. "No, I leave most of the heroics for you. But I wasn't about to let the two of them go alone when I learned you were in trouble."

Maksim chuckled. "Did you think I needed company in my prison?" He gave a single shake of his head. "I know you said you'd be willing to follow me anywhere, my love, but I think this is taking it a bit far."

Isha glanced around the room. "If the place was more than shadows, I might be able to figure out how true your words are."

"They're true," Kellan said dryly. "And you're probably better off not seeing the place clearly."

"They must have some sort of plan for everyone." Meikah tucked her amulet away. "Otherwise, why keep all of us alive."

"They're barely doing that," Maksim said. "One meal a day and it's a fight to make sure you get enough food. The ones who've been here the longest tend to end up with the least since they don't have the strength. Or at least that's the way things worked when I was thrown in here."

"What brought you here?" Kellan asked. "Why were you investigating the place?"

Maksim looked from Meikah to Kellan several times. "I take it you aren't asking out of curiosity."

"The Duke was concerned about your absence and asked us to deliver a message to the Commander of the Assassins Of The Dead while we were in Port Mayren," Kellan said.

"Why were you in Port Mayren?" Maksim asked.

"We'll tell you later." Kellan glanced at the room behind Maksim. "It looks like we'll have plenty of time to discuss everything that's happened since you left home."

"The Duke was informed of several people who went missing. When I tried to find out what had happened to them, it seemed they'd all travelled to Port Mayren and never returned. Following the very few clues I had, I started discovering instances of other people from other towns and villages who'd also gone missing when they travelled to the capital. By the time I reached Port

Mayren, I'd discovered nine people missing, all headed towards the capital."

"Did they reach Port Mayren?" Kellan asked.

"Some did, some didn't, so I searched the area outside the capital. In all, I'm fairly certain I can trace the death of thirteen innocent people to this village," Maksim said.

"What did each of them have in common?" Kellan asked.

"Absolutely nothing." Maksim slowly shook his head. "I learned everything I could about each of them and all I can think is that they were convenient. Different genders, different ages, different hair colour and different backgrounds. About the only thing they had in common was that none of them were wealthy."

"Convenient in what way?" Meikah asked.

"Wrong place, wrong time," Maksim said. "But that doesn't tell me why they needed thirteen people."

"There are a lot of dark spells that require the sacrifice of thirteen people," Kellan said. "I'm certain Hincke is a necromancer."

Maksim inclined his head.

"How many are in this room?" Isha asked.

"With the three of you, a hundred and twenty-seven," Maksim said.

"Is there a spell that takes that many people?" Meikah asked.

Maksim continued to hold Isha's hands. "There's a spell that requires a hundred and sixty-nine people."

"Thirteen times thirteen," Kellan said softly.

"Yes," Maksim said.

Meikah looked from Maksim to Kellan. "Is anyone going to tell me what the spell does?"

"It breaks down and destroys all the spells in a two-mile radius," Kellan said.

"Where would you use that type of spell?" Meikah asked.

"It would take out all the protective spells in any city of our country, as well as some of the areas outside the walls of the city," Maksim said.

"They're planning an invasion?" Meikah asked.

Maksim shrugged. "That's something I can only speculate on. Without more information, it's impossible to know what they're planning." He smiled wryly. "Gathering information is a little hard to do from in here."

"It's a good thing we didn't fail their test when they asked if any of us were a sorcerer," Kellan said. "I bet we wouldn't have been suitable if we'd said yes."

"Will that help?" Isha asked. "The two of you being able to use magic."

Meikah was relieved Isha didn't call them necromancers. Not that it made any difference in her ability to answer the question. She assumed it didn't help Kellan either since he shrugged.

"What is the routine around here? Can we see what's going on outside?" Kellan asked.

"There are a few places where there are cracks between the timber," Maksim said. "None of them big enough to get a good look at the village."

"What have you observed through them?" Kellan asked. "And where are they?"

"This way. I'll show you where the largest one is." Maksim let go of one of Isha's hands, keeping hold of the other one. He wound his way through the people in the room, heading for the back corner.

Meikah noticed some of the cracks between the timber that he'd mentioned, what little light there was in the room coming in through them. "Can any of the people in here see in the dark?"

"You'll become accustomed to the low light levels after a few days," Maksim assured her.

"That won't be necessary for the two of us," Kellan said.

Reaching the corner, which had fewer people in it than some of the other areas, Maksim studied Meikah. "What has happened while I've been gone?"

"I have no idea where to begin." Or more accurately, she didn't want to go over all the details about being a necromancer.

Maksim patted Meikah on the shoulder. "At the beginning, Meikah. That's usually the best place to start."

While Kellan peered through the cracks between the timber, shifting between several in the corner Maksim had led them to, Meikah briefly told her grandfather about the many changes that had occurred in the past few weeks, keeping her voice as low as possible when she talked about her new abilities. Talking about it made her realise it hadn't even been four weeks since she'd learned she was a necromancer. So much had happened in such a short amount of time. Her entire life had changed. And maybe not for the worse, like she'd originally thought.

Maksim crushed Meikah to him. "Nothing has changed. You're still the same person. All that is different is that you've discovered you have a few extra talents."

She returned his hug, shocked by how thin he felt. He'd never been a large man, but he'd always felt strong and solid to her. Now he felt fragile. She drew back from him, studying him once more. "We have to get you out of here."

Maksim smiled. "I nearly escaped when they first caught me. Got about a quarter of a mile from here before they captured me and brought me back."

Chapter Eight

Meikah smiled at her grandfather's words. "A farmer saw the guards bring you in here. It's how we knew where to find you."

Maksim chuckled. "I didn't make it easy for them." His smile faded and he glanced about the room. "We need to get everyone out of here. Whatever they're planning to do with the spell, it certainly won't be good or for anyone's benefit other than theirs."

"Are there as many guards patrolling the village of an evening as there are during the day?" Kellan looked up from the crack he peered through. "If there is, it's going to be impossible moving around the village to learn what's going on."

"There are about half the amount of guards of an evening," Maksim said. "But it's just as bright as they put lanterns out around the place when the sun sets. With the amount of fortifications and trained fighters, this is more than a typical village."

"How much of the place did you manage to search before you were discovered and how did you get in?" Kellan asked.

"They fixed the spot I came in through, an angled tree that I used to reach the outer wall, tying a rope to it so it'd stay in place and give me a way out. They've cut the forest back even further. And I didn't get very far with my search." Maksim crouched beside Kellan. "See that two-storey building with the extra guards out the front? That's where I think the leader lives and conducts his business. Hincke. That man oozes evil."

After Kellan had looked through the crack at the building, Meikah pressed herself against the wall to peer through it. "There has to be at least ten guards." They were never going to get inside.

"There are guards inside too. In the front room. Although like elsewhere in the village, there are less at Hincke's place of an evening," Maksim said. "The only time when there are even fewer guards is when they change over. It's all done at once. You have maybe ten minutes when everyone is on the move and it's possible to get inside."

"If they're all on the move, how do we predict where they'll be so we can get close?" Meikah asked.

"We'd need to be in place before they change the guards," Kellan said.

"I don't think you can use what few shadows there are to hide yourself. Many of them can use magic. I don't know how many of them are necromancers or if it's just Hincke who's one," Maksim said.

Meikah drew back from the crack between the timbers. No wonder people feared necromancers when there were ones like Hincke. She turned to Kellan. "What about Shade? Will he be able to help? And why can't the King just attack and free everyone here?"

"Any sign of the walls being breached and they'd slaughter all their prisoners and destroy any evidence of their plans," Maksim said.

"What if we coordinated it with Shade?" Meikah asked. "Have him arrange for the King to attack while we grab the evidence and set the prisoners free?"

"Few of this lot would be able to fight." Maksim made a gesture that encompassed the room. "They've been here too long with not enough food and stuck in the dark all that time."

Meikah's gaze travelled across the room. Not even the people nearby objected to Maksim's comment. In fact, most of them had their eyes closed and were slumped against either the wall or their neighbours. "Why do you have so much space?" She turned to Maksim. "You have this entire corner to yourself."

A young man huddled nearby looked up at Meikah's words. "He protects us."

Meikah frowned. "Protects who?"

"All of them," Maksim said. "I started with a few, but now most of them realise the benefits of working as a team. If we have the chance, we'll escape and each will be able to carry their own weight. Just not have the strength to fight."

"We need to get more food to them," Meikah said.

Maksim shook his head, a slight smile curving his lips. "It's a nice thought, Meikah, but it wouldn't help. They'd need more than a few days of decent food to be able to fight."

"Being able to walk out of here is a start," Kellan said. "If any of them had to be carried, that'd slow us down."

Meikah drew in a deep breath, trying to think of all that had to be done. "So we need to figure out what's going on and rescue everyone in this building. Including ourselves."

"Sounds about right." Kellan grinned. "Think you can strike a tree with lightning if I make it look like a storm is coming in tonight?"

Maksim looked Meikah up and down. "You can do that?"

"I don't know." She said the words slowly as she thought about it. "I've never done it before." But she had put her lightning into weapons. "How would I go about it?"

"Hurl all your magic at a tree and hope it works," Kellan suggested.

"That doesn't sound like a good plan," Meikah protested. "We need a plan that will work. Not one we're uncertain of." She sighed heavily. "What we need is Shade to set the place on fire. He could light one and use his wind to make it spread quickly. Then we could run around and find the evidence and get everyone out while they're distracted putting fires out."

"They're necromancers. They might have the ability to put fires out by using the moisture in the air. Better than Shade lighting the place up would be one of your dragons attacking and keeping them from suspecting they've been discovered," Kellan said.

"I don't know how to call them at will." Meikah's gaze was drawn to the back of her right hand. She didn't even know how to call the silhouette of the dragon to her hand at will. Not reliably. She really needed to learn more about being dragon touched so she knew what she could and couldn't do. Being able to call a dragon to help would have come in very useful right now. But she had a feeling dragons weren't anyone's to command. If someone was to do the commanding, it would be the dragon, not the dragon touched.

"Forget about the things we don't have. That won't help us come up with a suitable plan," Maksim said. "Focus on what we know and what we have."

"Are there any other exits out of this building?" Kellan asked.

Maksim shook his head. "One way in and out. It's also visible from three guard points."

"How often are the guards changed?" Kellan asked.

"Every six hours."

Meikah frowned. "There's no way we'll be able to sneak out of here, get in the other building and search it all within ten minutes."

"You'll have to do it over several guard changes," Maksim said.

"It's too dangerous," Isha protested. "If she's caught, they'll know she can use magic and have no use for her."

"It's not that they'll have no use for her," Maksim said. "It's that they won't be able to keep her imprisoned as easily."

Kellan peered through the cracks again. "Have you noticed any suitable hiding places while you've been here?"

"Straight out the door, two streets over, then turn left. There's a stable with a muck heap out the back. The area is less maintained and not many use it." Maksim chuckled. "For good reason."

"What about getting to Hincke's place?" Kellan asked. "What do you suggest about that?"

"Come in from behind his place," Maksim said. "I managed to search the bottom floor, but not the top. There are three windows across the back. Use the middle one. It's a storage room."

"When's the next change of guards?" Kellan asked.

"An hour or two." Maksim made a sweeping gesture to indicate their surroundings. "It's a little hard to keep track of time in this place."

Chapter Nine

"Will we have any warning they're about to change the guards?" Meikah wasn't sure any of the plan would work. It all seemed vague and not well thought out.

"We can keep watch and move the moment they begin the process," Kellan suggested.

"Surely you don't both need to go," Isha said. "Meikah could wait here with us."

"It might be harder to keep two of us hidden," Kellan said. "But having two of us searching Hincke's building will give us a greater chance of discovering what they're up to in the short time we'll have to search the place."

"Take your time," Maksim said. "Don't rush anything. If you don't manage to get into Hincke's place at the second change of guards, return to your hiding place behind the stable."

"Once darkness falls, I'll call up a mist to come in from the forest and into the village. Meikah can practice casting lightning in the sky. Then when we use a lightning struck tree for a distraction, it won't be unexpected," Kellan said.

"Want me to keep watch?" the man who'd spoken to them before asked.

Maksim didn't answer immediately. "Yes. Have everyone clear a path to make it quicker for the pair of them to reach the door. They won't have much time to get out of here once the guards start to move."

The man struggled to his feet, took one step away, then turned back to face them. "Is this it? Is this the rescue you told us to wait for?"

"It's one of the rescues I was expecting," Maksim said.

"A few of them said no one would find us here. No matter what you said about your people coming after you." The man smiled briefly, a crack in his parched lips splitting. Blood trickled down his chin. "I'm relieved to see they were wrong." This time when he turned away, he kept moving, occasionally bending to speak to those he passed.

Meikah turned to Kellan once the man was nearly at the door. "What if I can't throw my lightning at the sky?" She had no idea how to go about it.

Kellan grinned. "Then we better not take too long to find out what's going on."

"You can hide in the storage room once you're inside Hincke's place," Maksim said. "It's only when you leave the room that you need to be careful."

"How will we know they've made it safely to each of their destinations?" Isha asked.

"If mist forms tonight, you'll know we're safe," Kellan said.

Meikah didn't bother suggesting they keep an eye out for her lightning. She really needed to practice her abilities more. Her thoughts turned to Daveth and Marta. As far as she knew, they were the only people who could teach her how to use her dragon touched abilities. A pity they were both spirits and couldn't leave Durnning Island without no longer existing. And moving to the Arcton Mountains away from her home wasn't something she wanted to do. Especially since she had a feeling that being taught by dragons would be a very slow process. Most things were a slow process when it came to dragons. Unless one of theirs was in danger.

Isha reached for Meikah.

When her grandmother's attempt went wide, Meikah took hold of her hand. "You don't need to worry. I've faced worse than this." Surprisingly, it wasn't a lie. Life had been full of danger since she'd discovered she had the ability to be a necromancer.

"That doesn't reassure me, Meikie." Isha's grip momentarily tightened on Meikah. "Don't take any unnecessary risks and flee rather than stay to help us if you find you're outnumbered."

Meikah smiled, glad Isha wouldn't be able to see her expression. As if she'd leave anyone behind. And especially not someone who was family. "I'll be careful."

"Don't you go telling your grandmother lies like that," Maksim said.

Kellan laughed. "Isha shouldn't have expected anything else."

"Meikie, don't you risk yourself for us," Isha protested.

"It won't only be for you," Meikah said. "It'll be for everyone here and for those who'll be harmed by the spell if we allow it to be cast."

Isha half turned in Maksim's direction. "Haven't I always said she's a lot like you?"

Maksim chuckled. "Don't insult the poor girl like that, my love." He took Isha's hand from Meikah.

"I take it as a compliment," Meikah said. "I couldn't think of anything better."

Maksim drew Meikah close, giving her a one-armed hug, continuing to keep hold of his wife's hand. He pressed a kiss to the top of Meikah's head. "Do your best to come through this alive."

She was half tempted to point out that necromancers never truly died. They might lose their body, but they always lived. Of a fashion. Keeping the words to herself, she nodded, stepping back when Maksim let her go. "Is there anything else you can tell us about the village?"

They spent the next hour and a bit discussing every piece of information Maksim had gained about the village. There was very little since most of it had been through observing the place through the cracks between the timber and when he'd been sneaking in. Some of it they already knew, such as the regular arrival of supply wagons, but there were a few things they found interesting. Each morning Hincke rode off by himself and was gone for a few hours. He brought nothing back with him and took nothing out on his journey. Or at least nothing that Maksim had been able to see. Maksim hadn't been able to learn anything about where Hincke went and none of the villagers seemed to discuss it. Although none of the villagers seemed to talk about Hincke at all.

"That's odd," Kellan said. "None of them talk about him? Not even to complain?"

Maksim shook his head. "Either they're terrified of him, there are unknown spies amongst them, or they don't trust each other in general."

Meikah shuddered at the thought of Hincke's smile. "He probably terrifies them. Is there anything worse than seeing him smile?" She shuddered again. "We can't let him get away with whatever he's planning." She had no doubt it'd be evil and cause the death of more than the hundred and sixty-nine people he needed to create the spell.

"We'll stop him." Kellan met Meikah's gaze, his voice filled with grim determination. "We'll see that his plans fail and he ends up imprisoned as he deserves."

Before Meikah could reply, the man who was keeping watch joined them. "They've started."

With a nod, Meikah followed Kellan, who'd thanked the man before hurrying towards the door.

Isha and Maksim met them by the door, where Kellan was unlocking it with the help of his magic. Isha again reached for Meikah, who took her hand. Isha tightened her grip on Meikah. "Come back safely to us."

Meikah drew her hand from Isha's and threw her arms around the elderly woman. "Don't worry about me. Haven't you already said I'm like Grandfather Maksim? He always comes home to you."

"Eventually," Maksim said dryly.

Kellan opened the door a fraction. "Time to go. It's all clear." He turned to Meikah. "You head off without me. Keep close to the buildings and I'll catch up. I'll lock the door behind us so no one realises it's been opened."

Meikah drew away from her grandmother, smiling at Maksim, who rested a hand on her shoulder for a moment, the light a little brighter with the door open slightly.

"Run," Kellan urged. "Before it's too late."

With a glance outside, Meikah made a dash for the building across from them. Reaching it, she pressed herself against it, once more scanning the area for guards. There was one striding away from her and she followed him at a safe distance, pressing herself down low against the building when another guard turned the corner ahead of her and came onto the street. He greeted the other guard before continuing on his way.

Meikah held her breath, remaining against the building as the guard walked past her. Once he'd turned at the next corner, she let her breath out in a rush, drawing it in quickly as she realised he'd be walking past the building they'd been imprisoned in. Had Kellan made it to cover? Again she found herself holding her breath as she listened for shouts. Everything remained the same. Unnaturally quiet.

Until she'd stopped to listen, she hadn't realised how quiet the village was. In the distance she heard birds. Nearby there was mostly silence. Occasionally she heard the sound of a voice drifting her way, but there were no sounds of industry such as hammering. What did they do all day in the village other than patrol the streets and collect prisoners?

Chapter Ten

Relief rushed through Meikah when she spotted Kellan making his way towards her. Remembering his order, she scanned her surroundings before continuing along the street. The entire time it took her to reach the stable, Meikah kept expecting to be caught. She hid behind a couple of barrels that were beside the muck heap, relaxing back against the rear wall of the stable. On the other side of it she could hear the sounds of horses moving and the occasional soft whinny that was answered by a second and sometimes a third horse.

Spotting Kellan coming towards the muck heap, Meikah rose from where she crouched so he could see her. Crouching back down, she smiled at him when he joined her in the small space between the barrels and the wall. The ground was rocky and she could only assume it was the reason the barrels weren't pushed further back. She tried to get comfortable since they had six hours ahead of them before they could move again. It was impossible. Between the cramped space and the rocky ground, it was going to be a long day. Not to mention she was extremely aware of Kellan's body pressed against hers.

"You need to practice wielding your lightning," Kellan whispered.

She had no idea where to start. "How?"

Kellan grinned at her. "Haven't you learned anything from Amiel?"

A smile reluctantly formed. How many times had Amiel said something similar to her? Said in frustration, his tone filled with annoyance rather than the teasing Kellan's had contained. "Not according to him I haven't."

Kellan took hold of her hand. "Don't try so hard. Just immerse yourself in your magic and let it fill you. Learn the feel of it, the strength, the way it wants to behave."

She stared at him for a moment before she did as he said, letting the power of her magic rise and wash over her. Closing her eyes, it took her a moment to immerse herself in her magic rather than focus on his nearness. The sensation of her magic surprised her. How could something feel like it was both a part of her and separate to her? It was a strange sensation. The magic coiled around her, almost cat like, or possibly draconic in feel. Shock arrowed through her and her eyes opened. Was that the problem? Was that why she struggled to learn from anyone? Had the combination of being necromancer and dragon touched made her magic unique? She didn't know and now was probably the worst time to figure it out.

Trying not to sigh loudly, Meikah focused on her magic. Learning it, sensing it and trying to figure it out. She really needed to make time to learn how to use her magic properly. When all this was over she'd talk to Daveth and Marta and see what they knew about mixing the two. Although from the little the two spirits had said, she didn't think there'd ever been anyone who was both dragon touched and a necromancer.

By the time the day was drawing to a close, she felt like she'd gained very little understanding of her magic. Although she could describe very clearly what it felt like to be pressed against Kellan for so many hours. And she wasn't sure if she could cast lightning at the sky. The one thing she was certain of was that crouching for hours in a small space was one of the worst things she'd done. She'd have preferred to face a horde of zombies. At least she wouldn't have been tempted to press her lips to theirs.

Kellan leaned in closer, his lips near her cheek. "I'll raise a mist to close in around the village and slowly fill it."

She kept her head still, even though she was tempted to turn towards him. "I'm not sure I can cast lightning in the sky." Her voice was as low as his. "Or at a tree."

"If you can't, we'll come up with another idea when we need a distraction. Or search the place a few minutes at a time between guard changes."

She doubted she could manage too many more guard changes without needing a bathroom. As it was, she was hungry and in desperate need of something to drink. Obviously their planning had left a lot to be desired.

She went back to working with her magic and tried to put her lightning into the air like she did with weapons, but she had nothing to put it into. That was until she noticed the moisture in the air. Excitement raced through her when lightning forked through the sky, striking somewhere out of sight beyond the wall, the air filled with a crack of thunder as it struck. Grinning, she turned to Kellan. He spoke before she could say anything.

"I knew you'd figure it out."

"Just because I did it once, doesn't mean I'll be able to do it again," Meikah warned.

"Wait a bit before you try again," Kellan said. "We want the lightning to seem natural."

Meikah nodded, waiting what felt like a reasonable amount of time before she tried again. It took her a few minutes to manage, soon discovering that not all moisture in the air was suitable. It needed to have a certain amount of weight or density before she could use it. Another grin formed when a satisfying crack of thunder filled the air. She kept the lightning up, making sure the intervals between them were a similar length. She was so busy concentrating on her task that she was startled when Kellan pointed out the guards were changing.

Wincing at the pins and needles as she rose to her feet, Meikah stifled a groan. As far as she knew, there was no one nearby, but she wasn't about to take the chance.

"You go ahead. I want to count how many horses are in the stable. We're probably going to need a few to get some of the prisoners out of here that aren't doing so well. Just because they can walk doesn't mean they'll keep up with the pace we might need to set when we escape."

Meikah wanted to protest. Instead, she nodded. Some of the prisoners hadn't looked like they'd be able to go far. And certainly not make it all the way to Port Mayren. "Don't take too long." The thought of entering Hincke's place alone filled her with dread.

"It'll only take me a few minutes," Kellan assured her before moving away.

Meikah scanned her surroundings before heading towards Hincke's place. Along the way she cast her lightning at the air, not wanting to risk there being too much time between them. She arrived at the back of the building, having only had one close call, and pressed herself against the wall as she waited for Kellan. When it was close to ten minutes since the guards had started to change, she made herself crawl in the window of the storage room, climbing down off the crate she landed on.

The room was filled with crates, barrels and sacks. So there were plenty of places to hide. She peered out the window. She couldn't see Kellan anywhere. Before moving away from the window, she cast lightning once more. Had he been caught? He'd said he'd only be a few minutes. Catching sight of movement, she ducked below the window ledge when she realised it wasn't Kellan. She didn't want to be in here on her own. Kellan was meant to be with her. She sat on the floor, waiting a few minutes before she checked out the window again.

The guard had settled in where he stood, not far from Hincke's place, his back to the building. She didn't know where Kellan was or what had happened to him, but it looked like she was on her own. At least until the next guard change. Or longer, if he'd been caught. Hearing a sound outside the door of the storage room, she pressed herself into a corner behind two barrels, a sack lying across the top of them. The sound of footsteps continued on by. She remained where she was. Or at least until she remembered she was meant to be regularly making lightning fork through the sky.

Peering over the window ledge, she chose a point off to the side to cast her lightning. The crack of thunder filled the night. Should she have struck a tree? Was Kellan in need of a diversion? She couldn't do it straight away. Not without making the villagers wonder what was going on. Returning to her hiding place in the corner, she waited until a suitable amount of time had passed. About to cast her lightning at a tree out behind the building, she stopped. How was he meant to get in here if all the villagers went racing behind the building to see what was going on? Either this mission was more complicated than Tolmerr had expected or she wasn't cut out to be an Assassin Of The Dead.

Meikah cast her lightning at the sky, returning to her hiding place. What she needed to do was strike a tree towards the front of the building. She drew in a deep breath. But what if there was someone outside the storage room? She didn't know what to do.

Chapter Eleven

It took Meikah a few minutes to come to a decision. She'd see if anyone was on the other side of the door and then figure out what was the safest action. She opened the door a fraction at a time, first peering through the crack and then peering into the narrow hallway when the gap was wide enough. It was empty. She silently made her way to the right, planning to peer through the doorway of the closest room. She heard voices coming through the doorway before she reached it. Backing away, she turned and headed in the opposite direction, towards a set of stairs. There were two doors before the stairs, both of them closed.

Trying the first door, she found it locked. Before she had the chance to try the next door, she heard footsteps coming towards the hallway from the room she hadn't been able to check. Not wanting to risk finding the next door was locked and not having time to return to the storage room, Meikah headed up the stairs, relieved to find the hallway up there was empty. As was the first room she entered. It was a bedroom and was at the front of the building. Worried about how much time it had been since she'd cast lightning at the sky, she hurried to a window and struck a tree growing inside the village near the wall. Unlike outside the wall, all the trees hadn't been cut down in the village. The tree quickly caught fire and she turned away from it to survey the bedroom.

There was very little in the room other than a bed and a chest. No personal items, no decorations, and nothing had been left lying about. At least it made it simple to search the area. There was nothing hidden under the mattress, amongst the clothes in the chest or even under the bed. There was absolutely nothing of use in the room. Or nothing that gave her any idea of what Hincke and his people were up to. She returned to the door, that was closed, and pressed an ear against it. Everything seemed quiet in the hallway. Peering out, she found no one.

Meikah was torn. Should she search upstairs while it seemed quiet or remain hidden rather than risk being caught? What if things were quiet because of the burning tree? This might be her best chance to search the top floor of Hincke's place. In fact, it might be her only chance. Whoever slept up here would need to go to bed eventually.

Trying not to worry about Kellan, or anyone else for that matter, Meikah crept into the hallway. The three rooms at the front of the building were all bedrooms. Of the three rooms at the back, one was a bedroom, one was an office and the other was another storage room. She searched all the bedrooms first since they were as stark as the first one and easily dealt with. There was nothing of interest in any of them and she began to worry that searching them had been a bad idea. What if she ran out of time?

She stepped into the office. The desk was covered in letters, leather-bound books with scraps of paper jutting out of the top to mark places, pieces of paper with puzzling phrases and a map with various locations marked on it. Far too much for her to check through to discover what was important and far too much for her to carry. There were even several documents in the drawers, along with a nearly full bottle of scotch in the bottom drawer.

Leaving everything where she found it, she searched the storage room, finding a medium-sized cloth backpack in one of the chests. There was also a water canteen in the chest. Sadly, it was empty. Hearing voices coming up the stairs, Meikah scurried back to the office and stuffed everything in the backpack, slinging it into place as soon as it was crammed full. She froze when the voices stopped in the hallway outside the closed door of the office. The words were impossible to make out, only the underlying anger in the tone of one and the apologetic sound of the other. She couldn't stay in here.

Checking the window, she found it unlocked, but the climb to the ground wasn't going to be easy. About to climb out the window she thought of the empty desk behind her and returned to it, grabbing the scotch out of the bottom drawer and pouring it over the desk before returning to the window and half climbing out. She cast lightning at the desk, grinning when it went up in flames. Her grin vanished when she saw how quickly the fire took hold. She needed to get down to the ground before the flames reached her. Or the building collapsed.

She clung to the side of the building, trying to find another handhold. There appeared to be none. Drawing in a deep breath, she stifled a cough from the smoke billowing out the window. That had obviously been a terrible idea. But she hadn't wanted them to see the empty desk. Breathing in more cautiously, she struggled to remain calm as she scanned the back of the building for a way down. There was nothing. The only way was to let go and hope she didn't break anything when landing.

"What are you waiting for, Meikah?" Kellan demanded. "Do you want to burn alive?"

She looked down at the ground to see Kellan below her, Shade behind him standing close to the building set back from Hincke's place. "I'm stuck."

Shade came forward. "Put out the fires once they make large enough holes for her." He scooped up balls of fire from the burning house with gusts of wind and forced them against the wall beneath Meikah, making a track down to the ground.

Kellan put the flames out as soon as the fires had created large enough holes.

The process seemed to take forever, but Meikah guessed it was only minutes before she was able to climb down the back of the building. Voices rose loudly inside as someone yelled to fetch buckets of water while another argued other buildings were burning too and this one was too far gone to save. She stumbled as she reached the ground, her relief at reaching it quickly replaced by worry they might be caught.

Kellan drew her back from the building, wrapping his arms around her. "I couldn't believe it when I saw you clinging to the back of Hincke's place."

She clung to him, glad to be on the ground and even more glad he was unharmed. "I thought they might have caught you." She hated to think what Hincke would do if he caught either of them. He'd know they'd lied to him about having magic.

"We have to get out of here," Shade said. "Before the fire spreads too far."

Meikah drew back from Kellan to face Shade. "How did you get in the village?"

"Burnt a hole through the outer wall at the back of the village by setting a small fire at the base of it and using the wind to fan it higher." Shade smiled briefly. "It nearly got away on me, but I managed to put it out before anyone noticed it."

Before Meikah could ask Shade if he was unharmed, worried he might have some hidden injuries from breaking into the village, Kellan spoke to Shade.

"You unlock the door to the building the prisoners are kept in while I saddle horses. We'll meet at the stable." He turned to Meikah. "Want to help me?"

Nodding, she hurried to keep pace with Kellan as they went around the back way to the stable. "Shouldn't we be trying to avoid being spotted by guards rather than striding down the street like this?"

"Shade made the tree you set fire to burn more quickly and he caught the outer wall on fire too. The guards are busy trying to save the village." Kellan glanced at her, not slowing his pace. "Sorry I couldn't catch up with you. I couldn't get out of the stable. Two villagers stopped to talk to each other at the entrance."

"I was worried about you." She followed him inside the stable, glancing over her shoulder as she entered. "What if someone comes to get a horse?"

"They're all busy at the moment." Kellan grabbed tack and headed for the first horse. "That was a good plan, striking the tree when you did. A pity about Hincke's place catching fire before we could search it."

Meikah grabbed a bridle and went to the next horse, surprised to find it was one of the horses that had pulled their wagon. "I did search it. Hopefully, I took all the important information from it before I set the place on fire."

Kellan glanced at her. "You set it on fire?"

She nodded. "Doused the desk in scotch and struck it with lightning."

He chuckled as he put a saddle on the horse. "They should well and truly be kept busy while we get everyone out." He moved onto the next horse. "I was going to ask what you had in the backpack. I assumed you'd raided the storage room. I'm starving."

"So am I," Meikah said. "But I was too focused on finding information to think about it."

"Food will have to wait. Once everyone is safely away, we'll go after Hincke. Maksim can lead the prisoners to safety while we keep Hincke and his people busy."

Chapter Twelve

Finished saddling a horse, Meikah grabbed more tack. "We need people to help us saddle the horses. This is taking too long." She scanned the horses in the stable, spotting the other one that had drawn the wagon.

"Shade will bring everyone here soon," Kellan assured her. "What did you learn at Hincke's place?"

She shrugged as she started saddling another horse. "I didn't have time to look. There was too much and people were in the hallway outside the door of the room I was in."

"Doesn't matter. We'll check it over later. If nothing else, we know he's guilty of kidnapping."

Before Meikah could say anything in response to Kellan's comment, Shade came inside the stable. He stepped towards the side of the door, remaining against the wall. "Things are getting bad out there. We need to get everyone out as soon as possible. They've lost two buildings and another three have caught fire. They're likely to flee themselves. They'll start with the stables closest to the gates first, where most of the villagers are currently gathered, but they'll eventually come to this one."

Kellan kept saddling horses, only having glanced up when Shade entered. "Send a few of the prisoners in here to help saddle horses and you and Maksim check that the place where you entered hasn't been discovered so we can get everyone out of here."

With a single nod, Shade left.

Meikah didn't have time to finish saddling another horse before a dozen prisoners joined them, taking over the task. She left them to it, making her way to Isha, who remained by the door. "Are you unharmed?" She studied her grandmother, not seeing any wounds.

"I'm well, Meikah, but not all of those who were imprisoned are. Have you seen the wagon we brought with us? It would be good if we could cart some of them back to Port Mayren in it. They might be able to walk out of here, but I don't think they'll make it all the way back to the capital."

Meikah shook her head. She hadn't exactly been looking for it. "I guess it might be where they put it when they brought us into the village, but I don't know if that wheel will get it all the way back to Port Mayren."

"Did you want us to check to see if it's still there?" Kellan asked. "Even if it gets some of them halfway, it might help."

Shade joined them in the stable. "No time. We have to get everyone out of here now. Hincke has been calling his people together to give them orders to flee."

"We're done in here." Kellan nodded to the last of the prisoners, who was adjusting the stirrups of a saddle before swinging into it. "Is where you entered still undiscovered?"

Shade nodded. "Maksim has already started leading some of them there. We don't want to move too many of them at once. A large group might be noticed. I'll take another group over there and be back in a minute." He pointed to several of those on horseback before striding out of the stable, the ones he'd pointed to following him.

Meikah turned to Isha, taking off her backpack as she did. "Take care of this for me. We need to get it to Port Mayren."

Isha took the backpack, swinging it into place. "Why can't you take it?"

Meikah smiled. "We'll cover your retreat." She hugged Isha. "I'll meet you back at Garven's house. Don't wait around for us."

Isha tightened her arms around Meikah before letting go. "You better come home to us, Meikie."

She met Isha's gaze, seeing the worry clearly visible in her eyes. "I will." There was no way she wanted to end up as a spirit. She glanced past Isha at Shade, who'd already returned. "Now go. Before Hincke's people come here looking for horses."

There were still sixteen prisoners with them when three guards came to the fetch horses. The guards immediately reached for weapons. Two of them drawing swords while the third stayed back, readying a crossbow.

Meikah filled the swords with lightning, causing the two guards to drop their weapons. Before Meikah could do the same to the crossbow, the guards threw fireballs at her. She dropped to the ground, the fireballs going over her head. Remaining in a crouch, she scurried out of the way, not wanting to be set alight. Especially after escaping that fate earlier.

She watched the doorway of the stable, waiting for them to try and enter, Kellan on the other side of the door, crouched down low too. She wanted to ask him what they should do. There were prisoners in the stable with them that they needed to get to safety. A fireball came through the doorway, landing on some hay, flames leaping instantly upwards.

Kellan drew moisture from the air, putting the flames out. He'd no sooner extinguished them when more fire-balls came through the doorway. He dashed over to Meikah, crouching beside her. "Chase the last two horses out of the stable then get the prisoners out of here. Break through the back wall. I'll keep the guards busy."

She wanted to protest, but there was nothing she could do against fire. He'd already put out the new ones. Nodding, she chased the two horses out, watching as they raced along the street, avoiding being captured by the guard that reached for them. Trying not to think about returning to Port Mayren on foot, she scanned the stable to figure out the best place to break through the rear wall. She frowned as she pictured what had been out the back. Not wanting to end up in the muck heap, she headed for the opposite corner to it, gesturing for the prisoners to follow her. One of the prisoners brought a pitchfork.

"What are we going to do?" the oldest of the prisoners asked Meikah.

"We're going to get out of here." Meikah took the pitchfork from the prisoner who held it, using the tool to lever timbers away from the rear wall, forcing them outwards until they pulled the nails from the frame of the building.

"We can't go out there now they know we're here," another prisoner said. "They're all necromancers." There were murmurs of agreement from the rest of them.

Meikah grinned when Shade pulled away the plank she was levering off, glad his arrival gave her an excuse to ignore the comments. "This is the last of them. Can you get them out of here?" She helped Shade remove another plank so there was enough room for the prisoners to escape, one at a time. Behind her she could hear the crackle of flames as they flared up, then died away. She had no idea how long Kellan could keep the stable from burning down.

The moment the last prisoner had slipped through the gap, Shade had helped her create, Meikah ran to Kellan's side, avoiding a fireball. "They're out."

"We'll give them a minute, then follow," Kellan said.

"Can you keep this place from burning down for that long?" Meikah watched as another two fireballs took hold, a third one quickly following.

"Move to the other side so we don't get cut off from our escape and throw a few lightning bolts at them. We'll let the fire get going a bit to stop them from coming in after us." Kellan dashed to the other side of the doorway as soon as Meikah nodded.

She followed him, sending lightning at the ground in front of the guard she caught a glimpse of as she dashed past the doorway. "I can't see the other two."

Kellan peered around the door frame, drawing back when a fireball came through the opening. He glanced at the rear of the stable. "I can only see one of them. We'll go now. We can't let them go after the prisoners."

Meikah led the way to the broken wall, scanning the area outside before she slipped through the gap. The night was lit up by the burning village. She didn't know if she should feel bad about it or pleased they couldn't use the village to imprison more people.

Kellan joined her behind the stable. "This way."

Chapter Thirteen

Still scanning the area, Meikah followed Kellan. It didn't take them long to discover where the other two guards had gone. Shade fought them, the prisoners hiding in a single storey building behind him. He sent gusts of wind to send the fireballs they tossed at him back towards them. Meikah struck the ground in front of the guards with lightning, grinning when they dived for cover.

As soon as they had the chance, they joined Shade, the three of them retreating to the building where the prisoners peered out the windows. Kellan nodded towards the guards. "We'll keep them busy while you get everyone out of here. Join us once they're safely away."

Shade gave a single nod, leading the prisoners out the back of the building while Meikah and Kellan kept the guards busy.

Meikah threw another bolt of lightning at the ground when one of the guards started to come around the side of the building the two of them were hiding against. "How long do you think we need to do this? The fire is spreading really quickly." She didn't want to get caught in the village with no way out.

Kellan grinned at her. "I was going to say give them a few minutes, but that didn't work out all that well last time."

She reluctantly returned his grin, unable to resist even though she was worried about her grandparents getting back to Port Mayren and the three of them escaping the village before they were burned alive. "Should one of us go with my grandparents and the prisoners to make sure they get back safely?"

Kellan didn't answer straight away. "We'll send Shade with them and go after Hincke on our own."

She wasn't certain that sounded like any better of an idea. How long would it be before the entire village was on fire? "We could all go back with them."

"We can't let Hincke escape. Do you really think what we did here will stop him?" Kellan made a vague gesture encompassing the village.

Shaking her head in answer, Meikah struck the ground twice with lightning, once in front of each guard, the two of them trying to come around the building from opposite sides. Movement out of the corner of her eye caught her attention and she spun to face it, prepared to attack. She smiled apologetically at Shade, lowering her hands.

Kellan told Shade the plan and he left as silently as he'd arrived. The moment Shade was out of sight, Kellan turned to Meikah, who had regularly been throwing lightning at the guards. "We'll circle around and see if we can find Hincke."

Meikah struck the ground with lightning one more time before she slipped out the back of the building with Kellan, remaining silent as they moved away from the guards. The night had grown uncomfortably warm with all the burning buildings, the sky filled with plumes of smoke. A few times she had to fight against the urge to cough, but most of the smoke rose fairly quickly, a steady breeze blowing it upwards. She didn't know if it was a natural breeze or one created by the necromancers to deal with the smoke.

She waited until they were far enough away from the guards before she spoke. "Why haven't they used the moisture from the air to put the fires out?"

Kellan grinned. "Not everyone can do that. It's meant to be one of the more rare abilities amongst us. Fireball being the most common." He peered around the corner of a house. "There he is. Over by the main gate."

Meikah waited until Kellan drew back before she checked what was ahead of them. "How are we meant to get to him? There must be at least thirty of his guards around him, with most of them being mounted." She noticed there was another guard off to the side holding the reins of two horses. "We can't take on that many and hope to survive."

"We could follow him," Kellan suggested. "See where he's going and wait until he's alone or only has a few people with him."

Unable to think of a better idea, Meikah nodded. She kept close to the buildings, making her way towards the front gate and staying well away from the burning buildings. As they came closer, she noticed one man trying to put the fires out using the moisture from the air while the rest threw buckets of water on the flames.

The man turned away from the outer wall, facing Hincke. "It's impossible. If there were others of us who had the ability to work with water, we might have been able to save the place."

"I will tell you when it's time to give up," Hincke snapped.

"Yes, sir." The man turned his back on Hincke, his tone not sounding as respectful as his words.

"A pity we sent Shade to help get everyone safely back to Port Mayren. He could have made the wind pick up and fanned the flames higher," Kellan said. "Although from the way the wind is shifting, he'd probably be fighting against those who are manipulating it to keep the village from filling with smoke."

"Surely Hincke won't make them keep fighting the fire when they don't have the ability to use water." Meikah eyed the building that burned near the wall. At the rate it was burning, it'd collapse soon and some of the guards were far too close. "He's going to get them killed. Doesn't he care about his own people?"

"It doesn't look like he does," Kellan said.

Meikah looked at the tops of the trees she could see past the outer wall. "With how much ground was cleared between the forest and the village, I thought the fire would be contained, but from in here, the forest doesn't look that far away."

"Shade will let them know at Cryptic Ramblings. They'll send assassins to make sure it doesn't get out of control. It shouldn't with how much land is cleared, but they'll send them anyway so they can make certain."

Meikah was surprised at how relieved she felt. The last thing she'd wanted to do was burn down the forest. About to ask how much longer they should wait here, she stopped when Hincke spoke.

"Stay and work on putting out the fire. If you haven't got it under control by the end of an hour, join us at the northern village."

A woman tossed a bucket of water onto the fire before turning to face Hincke. "But my husband was sent to the eastern village."

Hincke looked her up and down. "Do you think you're above taking orders?"

She lowered her head, staring at the ground. "No, sir."

Hincke waited a moment before he turned to those on horseback. "Time to go. We need to leave in case the King sends someone to investigate what's happening here. The fire will be seen from miles away." He beckoned the guard holding the reins of the two horses, swinging into the saddle of the one handed over to him.

Meikah looked from the twenty guards left behind to the thirty leaving with Hincke. "How are we meant to get past these ones to follow him?"

"We could make our way back through the village and leave the way everyone else did," Kellan suggested.

She watched the orderly group ride away, the horses kept at a walking pace. "We better hurry then. And hope they don't go at a faster pace."

They retreated silently, making their way to the building where they'd found Shade earlier. Meikah scanned the area. The guards who'd been there seemed to have left. "Where to now?"

Kellan nodded in the direction he faced. "Shade went this way. It shouldn't be too hard to find where they went through the wall."

Meikah remained alert, constantly scanning her surroundings as they headed for the outer wall. She nearly ran into Kellan when he stopped, dragging her to the side and behind a building. "What-" She broke off when she caught a glimpse of a guard before she was pulled behind the building.

"The two guards we fought earlier," Kellan said. "They're at the break in the wall."

"We need to get past them." Meikah drew out of Kellan's grip and peered around the corner. Both guards held swords and one looked into the forest while the other scanned the village. There was no way past them without a fight. Movement caught her attention and she looked past the building on the opposite side of the street. The two horses she'd chased out of the stable were grazing on the other side of the street beside the building. She looked between the horses and the guards. There was no way they could cross the street without the guards seeing them.

Kellan pressed close to her to peer around the building. "I'll distract the guards while you get those two horses. If I draw the guards away from the opening, you can ride past me and I can get on the second horse. Make sure you come close enough to me I can grab the reins."

"You can't fight the two of them alone," Meikah protested.

Kellan grinned at her. "I guess we're about to find out." He drew his sword.

Chapter Fourteen

Meikah pulled Kellan back from the edge of the building when he would have stepped out into the open. "Are you trying to get yourself killed?"

"They both use fireballs. I can deal with fireballs. As long as you don't take too long," Kellan said.

"Are you sure?" She met his gaze, seeing the mist in his brown eyes.

Kellan gave a single nod. "You get the horses while I distract the guards. If we don't hurry, Hincke will get too far ahead and we'll have no hope of finding him."

Letting out a slow breath, she released him, taking a step back. "Be careful."

"I will." With another grin, Kellan stepped around the corner of the building and strode towards the guards.

Meikah stayed at the corner of the building, holding her breath as the fireballs thrown at Kellan went out with a sizzle before they reached him. Her breath escaped in a rush, relief at seeing him unharmed filling her. It looked like he could manage. She smiled when he stopped on the side of the road, feet spread, sword held ready.

"You're going to have to do better than that," Kellan called out. "Can you use those?" He nodded to the swords the guards held. "Or do you only know how to throw a common fireball?"

The guards shared a look before striding towards Kellan, attacking him the moment they were in reach.

Kellan met their attacks, blocking and slipping out of reach, moving so they moved with him, eventually turning their backs on Meikah.

The moment the guards had their backs to her, she dashed across the street, watching where she stepped so as to avoid making any noises. She slowed before she came close to the horses, not wanting to scare them. Speaking softly, reassuring the horses when they shied away, she grabbed the reins, needing to untangle one of them. "That's it. Easy now." She kept her tone soothing. "Ready to go for a ride?" She patted the horse on the neck before swinging into the saddle, keeping hold of the reins of the second horse.

She urged them forward, picking up speed as she headed towards the fight. Aiming for Kellan, she kept the horses at a steady pace as she came near him. When one of the guards turned towards her, she struck the ground at his feet with lightning. He jumped back out of the way, the horse prancing away from the fight.

Kellan ran towards Meikah, grabbing the reins and swinging into the saddle. A fireball barely missed him.

He was able to put out the next one cast in his direction. Leaning close over the horse's neck, he urged it forward.

Meikah followed Kellan, doing the same, trying not to think about the guards behind them that could cast fireballs. A sizzling sound had her checking over her shoulder. The air was heavy with moisture, fireballs spluttering out before they could reach them. After riding through the opening in the outer wall, she came alongside Kellan, sitting up now they were through the gap. "How will we find Hincke?" It had taken far too long to get past the guards.

"By hopefully not being so far behind that we'll be able to see him in the distance."

"And if we can't find him?" Meikah asked.

"We return to Port Mayren and go over all that you found in Hincke's place and hope there are some clues in it as to what he's up to and where we're likely to find him."

Meikah didn't like any of his plans. There were too many things left to chance. When they'd travelled twenty minutes down the road, without catching sight of Hincke and his men, she began to think the plans even worse than she'd initially thought. "We've lost him, haven't we?"

"Looks that way." Kellan glanced over his shoulder. "Hincke and his people must have turned down one of those narrower tracks. Or broke into a gallop the moment they were out of sight and are now way ahead of us."

"We could go faster," Meikah suggested.

Kellan shook his head. "We don't want to wear the horses out. Even if they aren't that far ahead, we also need to go to Port Mayren once we figure out where they're going. Thirty-one necromancers might be a few too many to take on."

"Only a few?" Meikah asked dryly.

Kellan grinned at her. "One or two."

She couldn't resist smiling at him. "If you say so."

His grin didn't falter.

Meikah glanced over her shoulder, wishing they'd caught up with Hincke. Kellan was right. What they'd done wouldn't prevent Hincke from going through with his plans. It would have only slowed him down. Not stopped him.

They weren't far from Port Mayren, a glimmer of daylight in the sky, when they slowed, a group of riders coming towards them. As they drew nearer, they spotted Shade at the front of the group, nearly two dozen Assassins Of The Dead with him. Shade drew to a stop when he reached them, his companions doing the same.

"You going back to the village?" Kellan asked.

Shade nodded.

"There were more than twenty guards when we left, but Hincke did tell them to leave after an hour if they weren't having any luck putting out the fire." Kellan grinned. "You and Meikah did a good job of setting the place on fire so I doubt they'd have put it out with only one necro capable of using water."

"Where did Hincke go?" one of Shade's companions asked.

Kellan shrugged. "We couldn't get past his guards to follow him straight away. We lost sight of him."

"We'll keep an eye out for him," the same man said.

When Shade started to ride off after his companions, who'd started forward again, Meikah called out, "Did everyone make it out?"

Shade nodded. "The prisoners were taken to the King and your grandparents went to Garven's house."

"Thank you." She returned Shade's nod with a smile, watching for a moment as he rode off.

"It'll be good to get back to my uncle's place." Kellan urged his horse forward, glancing at Meikah when she came alongside him. "I don't know about you, but I'm starving. Even more than I was before."

"I'm thirsty." If she'd have spotted a farmhouse along the way, she was certain she would have been tempted to visit in the hope of a drink and something to eat. Although if she had stopped, she might have fallen asleep with how tired she was.

"It won't take much longer to get to Uncle Garven's place," Kellan assured her. "Then we can have something to eat, sleep for a bit, then figure out where Hincke went."

By the time she saw Garven's house ahead of her, Meikah wasn't sure if she wanted sleep, food and water or to ask where the items were that she'd gathered. That was after she'd assured herself her grandparents were safe.

Isha came running out of the house as Meikah dismounted, wrapping her arms around her. "There's food ready for you in the kitchen. Come and I'll serve each of you a plate."

Maksim had also come outside, taking the reins of the horses. "I'll take care of the horses for the two of you." He looked both of them up and down. "You're looking as bad as some of those people we freed from Hincke's village."

Chapter Fifteen

Meikah wanted to protest, but with how she felt, Maksim was probably right about how terrible they looked. She used the bathroom before she made her way to the dining room where Isha had promised to have food waiting for them. After seating herself at the table and drinking half the glass of water placed in front of her, Meikah glanced around to make sure the four of them were alone. She turned to Isha. "What did you do with the backpack I asked you to bring back to the city?"

"It's in my bedroom." Isha started to rise.

Meikah waved Isha back to her seat. "After we've eaten will be fine." That was if she didn't fall asleep instead. Yesterday had been a long day and this one was looking like it might be just as bad. Even though it had barely begun.

"Are you certain, Meikie?" Isha asked.

"Once we've eaten," Meikah repeated.

When they had eaten, Maksim shook his head, placing a hand on Isha's arm when she rose to fetch the backpack.

"Let them sleep for a few hours or they're likely to collapse. They can go over everything once they wake."

Meikah tried to protest, yawning and stumbling as her grandfather ushered her to her room. Planning to rest for only a few minutes then search out her grandparents to say she'd been unable to sleep, Meikah fell into a deep sleep instead. She was woken around midday by Maksim who said he'd been going through the contents of the backpack.

"Is there anything of use in it?" She followed him to the dining room where everything was spread out across the table, Kellan already seated and going over a document.

Maksim shrugged. "There might be, but it's too early to tell. Mostly bits and pieces of information that we need more details about before we can make sense of it."

Sitting at the table, Meikah reached for the closest piece of paper, discovering it was a letter. She soon found out that Maksim was right. The bits of information she gained didn't make sense on their own. She was missing too many details.

Shade arrived after they'd been at it for a couple of hours, joining them in going over everything, accepting the offer of a late lunch, but declining the suggestion of having a rest as he'd dozed on the ride there and back. He'd informed them that no one had seen any sight of Hincke and the village had been empty when they'd arrived. The group of assassins he'd ridden out there with had remained behind to make sure the fire was contained.

Meikah read through more pages of correspondence, most of it related to supplies for building the village, the tediousness of it making her want to return to bed. Hoping for something more interesting, she reached for an aged, leather-bound book that was in the pile. It didn't take her long to realise it was a necromancer's spell book. She read over spell after spell, many of them needing human sacrifices.

Maksim looked up from the letter he was reading. "I know why they murdered the first lot of people. The thirteen that brought the village to my attention."

Meikah looked up from the spell she'd finished reading. "They made a tracking spell."

"How do you know?" Maksim asked.

Meikah glanced at the book in front of her, a scrap of paper having marked the page. "I've just finished reading over the spell they used." She shuddered. "They would have died in excruciating pain." She met Maksim's gaze. "We have to find Hincke. We can't let him do this to a hundred and sixty-nine people." She'd read that spell too. The one that destroyed all the spells in a two-mile radius. That page had also been marked.

"We will," Maksim promised her.

Kellan looked up from the map he was examining, comparing it to one he'd collected from the study. "None of these marks on Hincke's map correspond to anything marked on this one."

"They might be farmhouses or something similar," Shade suggested. "Things like that are never marked on maps."

"Unless they're famous," Kellan said.

Shade briefly smiled. "Or infamous."

Kellan chuckled. "Yeah. Exactly."

Shade rose and stood at Kellan's shoulder, studying the map. "Want me to check out some of these locations?"

"Let me make note of where each of them are first." Kellan collected pen and ink, marking the locations on the map from the study. "I'll give you twenty-four hours. If you're not back by then, I'll notify headquarters and request help to go after you." He pushed the map towards Shade.

"What order will you search them in?" Maksim asked.

Shade again studied the map, pointing out the order in which he'd visit the locations before striding from the room, folding the map and tucking it away as he went.

Meikah stared at the empty doorway. "Should we have let him go on his own? And what about sleep? A few hours of dozing on the back of a horse isn't enough."

Kellan reached for another piece of paper from the pile in the middle of the table. "He'll be all right. Until he joined us, he was accustomed to working alone and going on jobs where he needed to survive on little sleep for days at a time." Kellan turned his attention to the piece of paper in front of him, looking up from it almost immediately.

"They're going to use the spirits on Durnning Island for their army."

Meikah rose from the table, nearly knocking her chair over in her haste. "What do you mean?" She leaned closer, not waiting for his answer, and read the letter in front of him. "They're going to bind the dead to themselves?" Surely they wouldn't do that. Hadn't the spirits on Durnning Island already been through enough? "If the one who's bound a spirit to them dies, then the spirit will cease to exist too." She'd not long since read that spell in the book, along with all its warnings of what could happen to the spirit.

Kellan twisted in his seat so he could meet her gaze. "I know."

"We have to stop them." She dreaded to think what Hincke could do with an army the size of the one that could be created from the spirits on Durnning Island. That's why they'd originally been killed. To create an army of the dead. A shiver ran through her. An army to overthrow the King who'd reigned at the time. Was that what they planned to do? Overthrow Branok?

"If you want to go out there and prevent that from happening, I'll keep going through all of this and see what I can learn." Maksim gestured towards the middle of the table where everything they'd not got around to going through remained in a messy pile.

Meikah yawned, wishing she could sleep. Her earlier sleep hadn't been long enough. "We could ask Shorty to take us out there again."

Kellan slowly pushed his chair away from the table, giving Meikah plenty of time to get out of the way. "I can be ready in ten minutes." He faced Meikah. "Will that be enough time for you?"

She nodded, trying not to remember Daveth's pleas. He'd wanted to leave Durnning Island without ceasing to exist. She hadn't been able to bring herself to do a spell that would bind him to this world. Not that she'd known how to do one at the time. Before giving her grandparents a hug goodbye, she couldn't resist glancing at the spell book. That wasn't the case now. She knew exactly how it could be done. Pushing thoughts of necro-mancer spells from her mind, she returned to her room and readied herself for the trip out to Durnning Island.

By the time they reached Shorty's place there were only several more hours of daylight left in the day and Meikah was nearly falling off her horse. The earlier sleep felt like it had been an age away. She sat on the dock, waiting for Kellan to arrange another trip out to the island, falling asleep where she sat. The rocking motion of the boat woke her and she drew away from Kellan, who had his arm around her. "Sorry. I didn't mean to sleep."

He grinned. "I'm not complaining. And don't worry. You weren't the only one. I think I fell asleep the moment

I carried you on board and sat you down beside me, leaning you against me so you didn't fall overboard."

The rocking motion grew worse and Meikah looked up to see they approached the rocks that surrounded Durnning Island. She tried not to think about the coming visit. What would she say to the spirits when they asked for her help? This time she knew how to do a spell that would allow them to leave the island.

"We're going to have to set them free," Kellan said.

"What if they don't want to be set free?" Meikah asked.

He shrugged. "Surely that has to be the better option for them. Otherwise, they'll be forced to fight in a battle not of their choosing. Like they were being trained for back when they were killed."

Chapter Sixteen

Meikah wanted to protest. It felt like murder. But was it really when the spirits were no longer one of the living? "What if I can't bring myself to kill them?" Trying to kill someone who wasn't attacking her seemed wrong. Even if they were a spirit.

"They're already dead," Kellan reminded her.

"I know, but-" She broke off to shrug, not sure how to finish the sentence. No matter what he said, it felt wrong. They lived. Of a fashion.

Kellan took her hand, lightly squeezing it. "They might ask us to. You never know."

Meikah didn't think there was much of a chance of that. Not with how the spirits had tried to get her to bind them so they could leave the island. She rose to her feet as the movements of the boat calmed. Ahead of her was Durnning Island, a place she'd visited a few too many times lately.

"This is as close as I go." Shorty readied the rowboat, lowering it into the water for them.

Kellan climbed down to the rowboat first, helping Meikah down. He picked up the oars, nodding to Shorty when he warned them he wouldn't wait all afternoon. That he'd prefer to be home before sunset.

Meikah sat at the front of the rowboat, glancing skywards. They wouldn't have much time if Shorty was to arrive home before sunset. She scanned the shore as Kellan rowed towards the island. "Where is everyone? Each time they've been there waiting on the beach."

"They might have lost interest in us after how many times we've visited," Kellan suggested.

Meikah slowly shook her head. "I doubt it." Yet the shore remained empty. The moment they were close enough, she hopped out of the rowboat and helped drag it onto the beach. "It's too quiet."

"They took them."

Meikah spun to face Marta, relief rushing through her at the sight of the spirit. "Marta." She strode towards the dragon touched warrior. "Where is everyone?"

"Necromancers came here a couple of hours ago. I was at the cave, thinking about my life with the dragons." Marta looked out to sea, her voice lowering. "I knew there was nothing I could do. What can a spirit do against numerous necromancers?" She turned to Meikah again. "Even you, as untrained as you are, would be more than I could fight against. I could try, of course, but eventually you'd win."

"What necromancers?" Meikah asked.

Marta shrugged. "None of them called another by name. They knew what they wanted, and it was us. Each necromancer bound several spirits to them and forced them to return to the ship they had out past the rocks, needing to travel back and forth numerous times with their rowboats. It would have been easier for them if they'd bound us to weapons, but for some reason they chose to bind us to themselves."

"Was this man amongst them?" Kellan formed an image of Hincke out of mist.

Marta pointed at the misty figure. "He seemed to be the one leading them."

Meikah closed her eyes, trying not to think about what it meant, but she couldn't shake the dread that settled over her. Opening her eyes, she met Kellan's gaze. "We have to find him."

Kellan gave a single nod. "Maybe Shade will discover something. Or Maksim might have learned something from the rest of the papers you took from Hincke."

Marta stepped forward, grabbing hold of Meikah's hands. "Please, I beseech you. Bind me to a weapon and let me come with you. I would even be willing to be bound to one of you if, like the other necromancers, that is what you prefer."

"If we died, you'd die too." Kellan grinned briefly, one tinged with wryness. "Our body. If our body should die, then you would too. You can only be bound to something solid. Like a living human. Or an object."

Meikah tried to pull out of Marta's grip, but the dragon touched warrior was too strong.

"Bind me to one of your swords. Or your daggers," Marta pleaded. "Please. I would go with you to rescue Daveth."

Meikah wanted to look away from Marta's eyes that were filled with emotions, ones that made Meikah feel terrible for the spirit and wish she could help. It also wasn't like they could rescue Daveth either. Not without doing a spell she feared using.

"Sorry, Marta," Kellan said. "As tempting as it is to increase the power of my sword by binding you to it, it'd be wrong to use a necromancer's spell."

Marta let go of Meikah to grab hold of the front of Kellan's outfit. "I can help you capture the necromancers who took my companions from Durnning Island so they can't do this again. Please. Would you leave me here alone for an eternity? Haven't I suffered enough?"

"I can release you from this existence," Kellan offered.

"No." Marta drew back from him like he'd struck her. "Not until I know Daveth is no longer forced to do their bidding. I need to know he's been freed too. Or returned here."

Kellan slowly shook his head. "I'm sorry. That's not possible."

"Why not?" Marta demanded. "Aren't you necro-mancers?"

"I'm not going to take that path. Just because I have the ability to be a necromancer, it doesn't mean I need to become one," Kellan said.

"Then it was all for nothing," Marta said. "The years we were forced to endure this place, our deaths, everything. All for nothing."

"I'll do it." Meikah blurted the words out, unable to stand by and let Marta suffer after all she'd been through. "I'll bind you to my dagger."

"Meikah-"

She cut off Kellan's protests. "I know." She met his gaze, seeing the worry in his eyes. It reminded her of the worry she'd seen in Isha's eyes. "I know there's no going back. I know there's no set amount of using my necromancer abilities before they start to change me." Any spell might do that. Even the first. She closed her eyes, drawing in a deep breath before opening them. "But I can't leave her here. I can't let her suffer and I can't end her life. I'm not a murderer of the innocent."

Kellan came forward, capturing one of Meikah's hands. "Then let me do it."

She shook her head. "No. You declined. This is my choice. You've already made yours."

"I can't let-"

She pressed a finger to his lips, leaving her other hand held by his. "You can't stop me. You will not take my choice from me."

Kellan kissed the finger pressed against his lips before grinning at her, laughing when she hastily pulled both her hands away from him. "Let me share the burden with you then."

She again shook her head. "No, Kellan. My choice. Not yours." It wouldn't make things any better if they both did the spell, only risk them both changing.

"You don't know how to bind a spirit to you. Or to an object," Kellan said.

Chapter Seventeen

Meikah tried not to think of some of the spells she'd read in the necromancer's spell book. There were so many of them in it that she'd never use. She'd rather die first. "I know how." As well as far too many other spells, the words seeming embedded in her mind after reading them a single time. "The words are as clear as if the spell book was open in front of me."

"Yes." Kellan spoke softly. "It's like the spells themselves want us to use them." He paused a moment. "Are you certain, Meikah?"

She wasn't at all certain. In fact, she dreaded using a necromancer's spell. "It's the right thing to do." She turned to Marta. "I won't bind you to my body. I wouldn't have anyone tied to the life of it when I end up in so many dangerous situations." She drew her dagger and sword. "I offer you the choice of my weapons."

Marta ran a finger down the sword before lowering her hand and meeting Meikah's gaze. "The dagger."

"Are you certain?" Meikah asked.

Marta smiled, nodding in answer.

"What are you planning, Marta?" Kellan demanded.

Marta smiled. "If you gave me solid form with the binding, you wouldn't miss your dagger like you might miss your sword and maybe you'll allow me to wear the weapon of my binding at my hip rather than leave it at yours."

Meikah smiled. "I guess I'll need to get a new dagger." Not that she knew how she'd manage that since weapons made of night steel were uncommon and expensive.

"I have money hidden back home that you can have to replace your weapon," Marta offered. "It isn't like it's of any use to me these days."

Meikah took hold of Marta's hand. "You will have solid form when I finish binding you to the dagger. All will be able to see you and you'll be able to interact with the world around you. Yet when you need to, you'll be able to dwell in the dagger you're bound to, safe unless someone should completely destroy it."

"Meikah, no," Kellan protested. "Do a simpler spell. One that'll take less power."

"Does that mean I'll never be in spirit form again?" Marta asked. "That I'll either be solid or in the dagger."

Meikah ignored Kellan. If she was going to do this, then she'd do it right. She'd give Marta the life, of a fashion, that she should have been able to live. "Only if you choose. You'll be able to be in your spirit form whenever you wish."

"Meikah. Choose a lesser spell," Kellan insisted.

Again she ignored him, meeting Marta's gaze. "I'm sorry. This will hurt." At Marta's nod, she ran the tip of the dagger across the palm of the dragon touched, blood welling up while she held onto her. The moment she let go, Marta's wound began to close. She grabbed hold of her hand again and pressed it against the handle of the dagger. Blood dripped down the weapon, as dark as the metal it travelled across.

"Meikah." Kellan's tone was urgent.

When he reached for her, Meikah stepped to the side, shaking her head with a glance in his direction.

"Please, Meikah," Kellan said.

Closing her eyes, Meikah steadied her breathing. The words she needed filled her mind and she spoke them. She'd thought they might be difficult to pronounce, but they formed easily. Like she'd spoken them many times before. She was halfway through the spell when her right hand burned, the silhouette of a dragon in flight darkening against her skin. The heat travelled through her body and she struggled to speak the words, feeling like she was being engulfed in flames. A lacey dragon burst forth from her hand, flying up and growing in size, wings spread as it settled back down over the two of them.

The heat increased and Meikah could have sworn she could smell burning flesh, but still she pressed on, forcing the words out. The heat became unbearable and Meikah saw steam rise around them. Lightning played across her skin, a mix of whitish-blue and fire-red. It travelled across her hand and over Marta's skin.

The warrior threw back her head, a pain filled cry bursting from her.

Then the words were done and the dragon vanished in a burst of white light and red flames. Letting go of Marta and the dagger, Meikah collapsed to her knees, the dagger landing point first in the sand, the last of the lightning playing over the dark metal.

Marta fell to the sand in front of Meikah, breathing heavily as her knees collided with the ground. She met Meikah's gaze. "You should have told me how dangerous it was to you."

Kellan joined them, kneeling in front of Meikah who'd dropped down to sit on her legs, one hand against the sand keeping her upright. "Do you feel any different? Has it eroded away at who you are?"

Meikah had no answer for Kellan, so she kept her gaze on Marta instead, still feeling uncomfortably warm. "What makes you say that?"

"The dragon. It was protecting you. Or at least trying to protect you. For the heat to be so great and the dragon to be so large, you were in grave danger," Marta said. "I've only ever seen that great a display when someone was poisoned. And not by a mild poison either. By one that would take your life in seconds."

"Oh." Meikah tried to think of something else to say. Her mind was blank.

"Meikah?" Kellan's voice was soft as he reached for her, lightly brushing strands of hair back from her face. "How do you feel?" He frowned, pressing his fingers to her cheek. "You're hot, like you have a fever."

She reluctantly brushed his hand away from her face, his fingers having been cool against her heated skin. "I don't know how I feel." She felt hot, exhausted and empty. Like there was nothing left in her. Was that how it started? If it was, she'd rather remain in ignorance a little longer.

"Would you take a human life to create a spell?" Kellan asked.

"Of course not," the words burst from her automatically.

Kellan grinned, wrapping his arms around her and crushing her to him. "You're still you. Other than how hot you are."

"Can't breathe," Meikah protested, pushing against his shoulder.

He loosened his grip, but kept his arms around her. "When I saw that dragon, I didn't know what to do. For a minute I thought you would catch on fire."

Meikah didn't bother telling him she'd thought the same thing. "Are you sure I'm still me?"

"You didn't hesitate to answer me."

She drew back further so she could see him better. "That doesn't make sense. How can that tell you I'm still me?"

Kellan grinned. "You are definitely still you."

Shaking her head, Meikah pushed his arms away from her, stumbling to her feet. "You're not at all amusing, Kellan."

Chuckling, Kellan helped Marta to her feet, holding the dagger out to her.

Marta took a step back. "No. Not until Meikah has a weapon to replace it. I wouldn't want her to be without the means to protect herself."

Kellan held the dagger out to Meikah, glancing out to Shorty's boat. "We better get going before he leaves without us. I'm surprised he hasn't with how long we've been here. He's not going to get home before sunset."

Meikah sheathed her dagger. She'd get a replacement as soon as possible. It wouldn't be a night steel one, but she'd rather that the dagger Marta was bound to was in the warrior's keeping.

"Are we going after Daveth now?" Marta asked.

Kellan pushed the rowboat into deeper water, glancing over his shoulder before he answered. "We need to figure out where he is first. Where all of them are."

Marta joined Kellan, holding the rowboat while he climbed in. "How will we do that?"

Meikah followed them more slowly, feeling completely drained. Each step was an effort and she was tempted to remain in the water. Every part of her body was burning up. Forcing herself to get in the rowboat, she nearly fell into it.

Marta steadied her. "You are hot. That's not normal." Marta studied her. "Are you well?"

Chapter Eighteen

Meikah nodded, smiling reassuringly, Marta's hand cool against her skin. It felt like too much effort to speak and she had no idea if she was well. All she wanted to do was sleep and cool down. Sitting at the front of the rowboat, she kept her back to Marta and Kellan rather than face their scrutiny.

Shorty stood at the side of his boat, glaring down at them as they drew near. "Was about to leave you here. You told me you wouldn't be long."

Kellan went up first. "We didn't realise things would take so long."

Shorty eyed Marta up and down when she came onboard. "You didn't say nothing about another passenger."

Kellan helped Meikah come on board. "We didn't expect her to return with us." He faced Shorty once the rowboat was stowed. "Will that be a problem?"

Shorty didn't answer Kellan immediately. "Only charged you for two passengers."

Kellan tossed Shorty several coins, grinning when the man turned away. His grin vanished when Shorty reached the rear of the boat and turned to face them.

Meikah made her way to where she'd sat on the way over to the island, collapsing on the deck, sleep dragging at her. She tried to stay awake, wanting to talk to Marta, who sat near her. But it seemed that one minute she was staring at the approaching rocks and the next Kellan was shaking her awake and they were tied up at Shorty's dock.

She staggered to her feet, feeling disorientated and surprised to find the sun had well and truly set. No wonder Shorty had been annoyed with them.

She followed Kellan to where they'd left the horses, Marta remaining at her side. She looked from Marta to the horses. "You can ride with me if you want."

Marta nodded. "I'd appreciate that." She mounted behind Meikah, her hands resting on Meikah's hips. "At least you're no longer hot now."

Meikah nodded, not having realised until Marta had pointed it out. She was still struggling to shake the last shreds of sleep from herself. She could have done with a few extra hours.

The trip back to Garven's was filled with comments from Marta on how much everything had changed and questions about what had happened to some of the buildings she'd once known. Meikah hadn't been able to tell her anything since this was the first time she'd been to

Port Mayren and Kellan had only been able to answer some of the questions.

They arrived at Garven's at the same time as Shade, who greeted Marta since he'd met her when he'd been on Durnning Island. The four of them made their way to the dining room where Maksim was reading over the information that had been left in there. He looked up as they entered. "I hope the three of you had better luck than I've had." His gaze rested on Marta. "Four of you?"

"This is Marta," Meikah said. "She's a spirit."

"A spirit I can see," Maksim said.

Meikah nodded, not sure she should answer the questions she heard in his tone. Would he look at her differently if he knew she'd cast a necromancer's spell? She turned to Shade instead of answering. "Did you find out what's at each of the marks on the map?"

"Mostly." He spread the map out on the table. "This one is the village we burned." He pointed to one of the marks on the map. "These three are also villages." Again he pointed to marks. "Ones that have been built during the past several months and have tall outer walls surrounding them." He slid his finger across the map. "And this one seems empty."

"You didn't see anything there at all?" Kellan asked. "Did you check the trees? Look for caves?"

Shade nodded. "If there's something there, it's well hidden." He glanced at Marta. "Did you discover anything other than a spirit?"

Kellan also glanced at Marta. "Nothing we were hoping to discover. We were expecting an island full of spirits. Marta was the last one there. Hincke now has an army." He explained what had happened, with Marta adding a few extra comments.

"That makes a lot of sense since there are a few letters Hincke has exchanged with someone talking about setting their grandfathers free," Maksim said.

"Where do they plan to attack?" Meikah asked.

"That's what I can't quite figure out," Maksim said. "They used the initial spell on a fellow necromancer who allowed himself to be captured so they could track him down. The thirteen who were killed were used to create a spell that can track someone past any spells that would normally conceal them."

"If they have an army, why do they need to do the spell with the hundred and sixty-nine people?" Meikah asked.

"Because wherever it is they're attacking, they'll need more than an army to get past the spells. One of the reports talks about all the spells that need to be broken. The place is heavily guarded and nowhere I know of. I know the spells of every prison and the list doesn't match any of them," Maksim said. "And if their grandfathers have been unlawfully imprisoned, then whoever is keeping them must be extremely powerful considering some of the spells used."

"Maybe Tolmerr might know where their grandfathers are being held prisoner," Kellan suggested. "We'll need to give all this to him soon, anyway."

Meikah wanted to protest. What if there were more details they could learn from it? Instead, she forced herself to nod. "When?"

"Could I visit this Tolmerr with you?" Maksim asked.

"I can ask, but I doubt he'd allow that," Shade said.

"Asking might slow everything down." Kellan turned to Marta. "You won't be allowed to come with us either."

"Can I wait here?" Marta asked.

Kellan nodded. "I'll let the housekeeper know you're staying with us and she can show you to a room."

"That won't be necessary. I have no need of sleep," Marta said. "I'll wander around in the night rather than take up a room that might be needed for someone else."

It took Kellan a few minutes to convince Marta it'd be less trouble if she had a room and it'd be best not to let the housekeeper know she was a spirit. When he went to introduce her to the housekeeper, Meikah went with him in search of Isha who Maksim had said was in the kitchen.

Isha hurried to Meikah the moment she entered the kitchen, holding her tight. "When did you get back? I've been worried about you."

Guilt struck Meikah. She should have let Isha know the moment she'd returned. "Sorry. We were sharing the information each of us had learned."

"I understand, Meikie. Haven't I lived with Maksim all these years?" Isha smiled. "I know you have important work to do."

"We're going out again. We need to deliver the backpack contents to someone." An urge to keep the necromancer's spell book filled Meikah and she pushed it aside, fear racing through her on the heels of that impulse. What if Kellan was wrong? What if she really was becoming a necromancer? Why else would she want to keep the spell book since she'd read every page and now knew all the spells? Even the one she'd cast on Marta. It seemed once learned, you could recall them to use again.

"What about dinner?" Isha asked.

"We'll be back for dinner. It shouldn't take us too long." Or at least Meikah hoped it wouldn't. They needed to find Hincke before he let his army loose on someone. Or some place.

Reaching Cryptic Ramblings, Meikah stepped back out of the way as two assassins exited. She turned to stare after them, waiting until they were far enough away not to hear before she spoke. "They're spirits?"

Kellan grinned. "You didn't think dying would get you out of being an assassin, did you?"

Meikah shrugged. "I hadn't really thought of it."

Shade held the door open of the bookshop, entering once the two of them were inside. "There are quite a few assassins who are spirits. They tend to go on the more dangerous missions." He closed the door and strode ahead of them, leading the way to Tolmerr's office where their way was blocked by a young man.

The three of them struggled to convince him they had important business to discuss with Tolmerr. It was a different assassin to the one who'd been standing on guard at Tolmerr's door when they'd been summoned to see him.

The young man crossed his arms over his chest, blocking their way. "You'll have to return tomorrow."

"Let him know a group of necromancers have raised an army of the dead," Kellan said.

The young man smirked. "Sure they have. We've made certain all the dead around here can't be raised."

"What about the dead on Durnning Island?" Meikah asked.

"No one goes out there," he protested.

Chapter Nineteen

Meikah fought the urge to push the young man aside and burst into Tolmerr's office. "We've been out there." They didn't have time for this.

"What have you been out there for?" the young man demanded.

Meikah suppressed a sigh of frustration. How were they meant to convince him how serious the matter was?

"Tolmerr was the one to send us on a mission," Kellan said. "Maybe you better let him know we've returned. Do you need us to repeat our names?"

"I was told he wasn't to be bothered except in an emergency and nothing was said about Tolmerr waiting on a report. So it can wait until the morning," the young man stated.

"This is an emergency," Meikah said.

The young man uncrossed his arms. "Look-"

Fed up, Meikah interrupted him. "No, you look." She stepped forward, seeing the lightning in her eyes reflected back at her from the young man's eyes. "Tell Tolmerr we're here. Tell him an army of the dead has been raised and tell him we need to see him now." She wasn't about to let Hincke attack anyone if she could help it. "And if he can't see us in five minutes, I'll be taking what we've learned to the King. I know he'll see me."

Kellan chuckled. "Considering you're on a first name basis with him, of course he'll see you."

Anger rushed through Meikah at the speculative look that crossed the young man's face. Before she could correct his impression, he turned away.

He glanced over his shoulder as he rested his hand on the doorknob. "Wait here." He swung open the door and slipped inside.

Meikah turned to Kellan. "Will you stop saying that all the time?"

Kellan grinned. "It seems to make things happen."

Shade placed a hand on Meikah's shoulder, pushing her back a step from Kellan. "You might want to look a little less angry before we see Tolmerr. You also might want to release some of your magic. From the look of you, anyone would think you're about to attack someone."

Considering she felt like attacking someone, particularly anyone preventing her from finding Hincke, she couldn't exactly argue Shade's comment. Breathing out heavily, she turned away from the two of them in time to see the door open and the young man stand to the side so they could enter. Spotting a dagger at his side, she smiled at him as she stepped past him, feeding some of her lightning into the dagger. She regretted it the moment she'd done it, worrying the earlier spell had changed her. Was she becoming a necromancer? How could she know? Was there a test? Could anyone tell? She hadn't realised she wouldn't know for certain. She'd thought it would be a simple matter of telling if she'd become a necromancer.

Tolmerr was seated behind a desk, a plate of half-eaten food to his right, a stack of papers in front of him. The pile of papers that was face down to the left of him was far lower than the one in front that needed his attention. He signed the piece of paper on the top of the stack in front of him and set it face down on the pile to his left before looking up. He gave the young man in the hallway a nod and waited until he'd closed the door behind him before he spoke. "This better be important. As you can see my meal is going cold and I have more work than I can complete today."

Shade held out the folded map. "We were wondering if you know what's at the marked location we've circled."

"You've wasted my time to ask about locations?" Tolmerr demanded.

Meikah took the map from Shade, unfolding it and holding it up so Tolmerr could see what Shade had referred to. "Hincke has raised an army of the dead and that's the only location on his map that doesn't make sense. The rest are villages of what we believe are necromancers."

Tolmerr stilled. "Give me a full report."

Meikah studied Tolmerr. "It means something to you."

"Give me a full report." Tolmerr said the words more firmly this time.

Kellan stepped forward, shifting Meikah to the side in the process. "Yes, Commander."

Meikah impatiently listened to Kellan's report as he handed over the backpack, wishing he'd hurry and that he hadn't bothered with so many details. They needed to find out why this location was important to Hincke and if it was where he was likely to go next. With his army of the dead. The moment Kellan was finished, Meikah blurted out, "What is at that location?"

Tolmerr rose to his feet. "I'll take things from here. You've done a good job."

Meikah stared at him open-mouthed. He was dismissing them? She closed her mouth, her eyes narrowing as she turned to Kellan. "We should have gone to Branok. At least he didn't push us aside and actually let us help him."

Kellan grinned. "Now who's mentioning the King by his first name? It's not like your dragon is around to hear you call him King."

"Mezeth isn't my dragon," Meikah protested.

Tolmerr looked from one to the other, his gaze coming to a rest on Kellan. "Did you leave details out of your report?"

Kellan shook his head. "Not regarding this matter. We're talking about the matter that brought us here, Commander."

Tolmerr turned to Meikah. "How quickly can you gain an audience with the King?"

She shrugged. "I don't know."

"The last one was within minutes," Shade said.

This time Tolmerr looked between the three of them, his gaze coming to a rest on Meikah. "You had best be telling the truth. We don't have an hour to wait for the King to see me." He gestured towards the door. "Lead the way."

Not knowing what else to do, Meikah did as Tolmerr had ordered. She made her way to the castle, her pace brisk as she worried that the King wouldn't bother to see her now the dragon was no longer a problem.

Kellan strode beside her, Shade and Tolmerr following them. He leaned close, keeping his voice low. "Tolmerr is nothing like Danton. To him we're low level assassins and most of the time not worthy of high level assignments. If you don't manage to get us in to see the King, he'll ship us home and we won't be able to help stop Hincke."

"He was the one who sent us to find Maksim," Meikah protested.

"When he thought it was just a missing agent of the Duke. Now it's something more. I don't know what since we don't have all the information, but if we can't get him in to see the King in well less than an hour, then we'll be sent home like a handful of children who were underfoot. They have more assassins than we do in Dreyton and won't have to resort to using partially trained ones."

Meikah wanted to argue with Tolmerr that she deserved to be a part of bringing Hincke down. They were the ones who'd discovered what was going on. She'd been the one to gather all the evidence and with Isha, Maksim, Kellan and Shade's help they'd brought it back to Port Mayren. "The King better see me in less than half an hour or I'll be using Mezeth's name to hurry him up." Not that she was certain that'd be enough to gain an audience with him. But she wasn't about to let their mission be given to others. That wasn't in the slightest bit fair.

Instead of going to the front entrance, Meikah headed to where they'd been taken when they'd first come to Port Mayren, relieved to recognise the guards on duty. She smiled at them. Hopefully, it meant she wouldn't have to convince them to take a message to the King for her.

One of them shifted uncomfortably. "I suppose you want to see the King."

Meikah nodded. "Tell him it's urgent."

The other guard tried to hide a smile. He wasn't very successful. "I'll let him know." He turned away, striding from them.

Chapter Twenty

Meikah fought the urge to call after the guard and tell him he had no idea what was going on. She remained silent, ignoring the speculative looks Tolmerr was giving her. She didn't know what was worse. Whatever they might be thinking or being sent home and not finishing what they'd started. She kept her gaze away from Tolmerr, determined not to let his speculative looks bother her. This was too important. She thought of Marta, who desperately wanted to help free Daveth from Hincke's control. It was important to more than herself. She'd weathered rumours before. She could certainly do it again.

The guard returned, beckoning them to follow. Meikah was surprised he led them to a sitting room where the King was being shown two outfits, shaking his head at both of them. He looked past Meikah to Tolmerr. "Was this a ploy to avoid protocol? Are you using your assassins to gain an audience more quickly than our agreement dictates?"

Not wanting to risk being unable to see the King so quickly in case she had need to again, Meikah held the map out to him. "What is at this location?" She pointed to the mark that had been circled.

Branok took the map from her, sending the servant from the room, his gaze remaining on Meikah. "Where did you get this?"

"From a necromancer who's raised an army of the dead and is trying to create a spell that breaks down and destroys all the spells in a two-mile radius," Meikah said. "All we really know is that he's trying to free his grandfather."

Branok made his way to one of the two armchairs in the room, sitting heavily. "Do you remember the necromancers who tried to overthrow my grandfather Timell?"

Meikah nodded. They'd nearly won. That wasn't something she'd easily forget.

Branok pointed to the circled mark on the map. "That is where they're imprisoned. Where all necromancers are imprisoned. In an underground prison guarded by numerous spells and guards who never leave the place so as to make it impossible for anyone to find."

Kellan came forward. "They sacrificed one of their own to be captured and imprisoned so they could learn where it is."

"How big is their army?" Branok asked. "And what type of dead?"

"Spirits," Meikah said.

At the same time, Kellan also spoke. "Hundreds. All the spirits from Durnning Island."

Meikah almost said it was all the spirits except one. She kept the words to herself. Would they hold any of this against Marta if they learned she was one of the spirits from Durnning Island?

Branok turned to Tolmerr. "You know my men can't fight spirits."

"They can fight necromancers," Tolmerr said.

"How many do you need?" Branok asked.

"Fifty should be enough from what my people said were living at the village that burned," Tolmerr said.

"There are four villages in total," Meikah said.

"That is speculation," Tolmerr said. "You have no proof those other villages are part of this plot."

Meikah faced Tolmerr. "Are you going to take that chance? Why not ask to have four times the amount of soldiers in case it's more than speculation?"

Tolmerr nodded towards Branok, his gaze remaining on Meikah. "Will you repay the favours that would incur? Fifty soldiers will be bad enough."

Meikah looked from one to the other, glaring at Kellan when he tugged her back before she could barely make a sound.

Kellan stepped in front of Meikah. "She's still learning the ropes. She doesn't understand how things are done."

Meikah glared at Kellan. "I might not understand how things are done, but I do understand what happens when you send too few soldiers into a battle. They get slaughtered and can be used to increase the size of a necromancer's army."

Branok nodded thoughtfully. "She has a point."

Meikah pushed Kellan's hand away when he tried to stop her from speaking again. She met Branok's gaze. "You said you owed me a debt. Use it to provide enough soldiers so they won't die to a necromancer's army."

"Are you certain that's how you want me to repay you?" Branok asked.

"Yes. Send as many soldiers as you can," Meikah said.

"Four hundred," Branok said.

She smiled. Hincke wouldn't be able to escape from that many soldiers. "Thank you."

"If that is all, I have a state dinner to dress for," Branok said.

Meikah nodded.

Branok turned to Tolmerr. "I'll send word to the barracks. They'll be ready within the hour."

"I appreciate that, Branok." Tolmerr glanced at the garments the servant had left behind. "I'll leave you to your preparations."

Meikah followed her companions to the door, the last to reach it.

"Meikah."

She turned to face Branok, surprised he'd called her name. "Yes?"

"Most would have requested something for themselves."

She held his gaze for a moment before shaking her head. "Not everyone." When he inclined his head, she hurried after her companions, not wanting to be left behind since she had no idea how to find her way out of the castle.

Tolmerr returned to Cryptic Ramblings, giving orders for all trained assassins to prepare for battle. Those who weren't fully trained were to remain behind. He halted Meikah, Kellan and Shade when they started to leave. "Those that aren't fully trained includes the three of you. Either remain here or return to where you're staying."

"You're going to make us stay behind after I used my favour with the King to get the soldiers you need?" Meikah couldn't believe he'd do that. She'd been certain he'd let them go with him. "This is our mission. We found out what was going on."

"And you'll receive a commendation for your work in this matter," Tolmerr said. "But it's now more complex than I initially believed and must be dealt with by highly experienced assassins. Not ones who are still being trained."

Meikah's hands curled into fists. "I don't want a-"

Kellan interrupted her. "We'll return to Garven's, sir. Send word to us there if you have further need of us." He pulled Meikah towards the exit.

She tried to shrug him off. "But I don't-"

Again Kellan interrupted her. "There's no point sticking around here. I'm sure you'd rather spend time with your family than sit here waiting to find out what's happening."

It wasn't until they were outside that Meikah was finally able to pull out of Kellan's grip. "I can't believe you did that. How could you-"

Kellan clamped a hand over her mouth, pressing his cheek against hers as he whispered to her. "It's better to go ahead and seek out forgiveness later. We can say we wanted to watch from a distance, but got drawn in."

Meikah drew back enough to meet his gaze, dragging his hand away from her mouth. "We're go-"

Kellan clamped a hand over her mouth again. "Hush. Before someone locks us in a room for the night and then we won't be able to help." He grinned. "Or get in the way."

Dragging his hand away from her mouth again, she glanced over her shoulder at Cryptic Ramblings. "Would they lock us up?" She kept her voice low.

Kellan laughed. "They would and they have. Now let's get out of here."

Chapter Twenty-One

Meikah found herself regularly checking over her shoulder all the way back to Garven's house, half expecting to find Tolmerr coming after them to lock them away so they couldn't follow. They were barely inside the house when Maksim met them.

"Did you discover what the location is?"

Meikah nodded, glancing past her grandfather to where Marta stood before she explained what had happened.

"They're not going to let you go after all you've done to help?" Maksim demanded indignantly.

Kellan grinned. "No, but that's all right. We'll find a quiet spot where we can watch what's going on at a distance."

Maksim chuckled. "Let me guess. Somehow or other you'll probably end up being dragged into the fight."

Kellan shrugged. "It happens from time to time. I can't be expected to judge where a battle might end up."

"I'll organise horses." Maksim strode outside before anyone could comment.

Meikah took a step towards the front door, halted by Kellan drawing her back. She tried to shrug out of his grip. "He needs to rest. He shouldn't be going with us. Not in his state."

"Like we shouldn't be going with our limited skills?" Kellan asked.

Meikah started to argue again, sighing heavily instead. "I just don't want anything to happen to him."

"He deserves to see this through as much as we do," Shade said. "More than we do."

She nodded, even though she didn't like the idea.

"Your grandmother has food ready for you," Marta said. "She told me to let you know when you returned, but I hated to interrupt."

"We'd best eat," Kellan said. "Who knows when we'll get the chance."

They left the moment they'd finished eating, the five of them riding in the direction of the underground prison. Meikah sent frequent glances towards her grandfather, relieved to find he was holding up better than she'd expected. A couple of times they had to skirt around soldiers and assassins, but they arrived at a point overlooking the spot marked on the map without being caught and sent home.

Meikah dismounted, tying her horse to the low branch of a tree before moving forward to peer at the necromancers, the army of the dead and the prisoners gathered amongst the trees. From what she could see, she had to guess that Hincke had gathered a hundred and sixty-nine prisoners and the same amount of spirits each held a dagger at the throat of a prisoner. They all looked at Hincke, who stood in a recently created clearing, talking about how they'd teach a lesson to all those who'd ostracised and oppressed them.

Marta grabbed Meikah's arm, pointing off to the right. "There's Daveth."

Meikah stared at the familiar spirit. Like the rest of them, he held a dagger at the throat of a prisoner. A dark haired young man wearing faded clothes. A glance around showed that most of the other prisoners were similarly garbed. "He's captured the poor and destitute."

"No one will immediately miss them," Maksim said.

"We can't let them be killed," Meikah stated.

"If they don't have all the prisoners, the spell won't work," Kellan said. "It'd be pointless for them to kill everyone when they'd only need to gather more before they could attempt the spell again."

"I can sneak up to Daveth in spirit form and drag him further back into the trees so you can take his prisoner," Marta suggested.

They discussed it amongst themselves for a few minutes, refining the plan. Marta became hazy, still visible to those who could see the dead, but less noticeable than if she was in solid form.

Meikah followed the dragon touched warrior, keeping back so she wasn't noticed by the necromancers. Kellan had said that unless the spirits had been given the command to let anyone know they were there, they'd remain focused on keeping hold of their prisoners. She could only hope he was right. When Marta grabbed hold of Daveth, clamping one hand around his mouth and the other around his wrist to keep him from killing the prisoner, Meikah held her breath, ready to help as soon as Marta had dragged him far enough back from the spirits that had been standing a few feet to either side of him.

She let her breath out in a rush as Marta drew near, grabbing hold of Daveth while Shade and Maksim took the prisoner from him. She met Daveth's gaze, struggling to hold on to him while Marta kept her hand clamped over his mouth so he couldn't let anyone know they were there. "Can you fight it?"

Daveth shook his head, trying to pull Marta's hand from his mouth, Kellan having taken the dagger from him. He tried to speak, but his words were impossible to understand.

"If we let you go, will you attack us or let Hincke know we took his prisoner?" Meikah wanted to glance over her shoulder to see if Shade had left, taking the prisoner to safety, but she didn't dare take her attention off Daveth. Not with how difficult it was to keep him from escaping.

Daveth again tried to speak, Marta preventing him from making more than unintelligible sounds.

"Nod if you'll attack us, shake your head if you won't," Kellan said.

Daveth nodded, again trying to speak.

Meikah wanted to close her eyes, rather than look into Daveth's. They were filled with anger, desperation and pleading. She didn't want to harm Daveth. "Can spirits be tied up?"

"No," Kellan said. "The moment one of us let him go, he'd be able to escape."

"We need to do something quickly," Maksim warned. "It sounds like Hincke is getting ready to kill his prisoners."

Before Meikah could say anything, the sounds of fighting broke out in the distance and Hincke called for order. "Keep Daveth from escaping." She glanced at each of her companions, letting go of Daveth the moment Kellan and Maksim also had hold of him. "Keep him safe." She strode towards the clearing, the sounds of fighting coming closer. "Hincke!"

He looked in her direction. "You're a fool coming here. I could order your death in seconds."

She kept her distance from the spirits and necromancers. "We've set free one of your prisoners. The spell won't work."

Hincke grinned. "You think that will stop me?" He grabbed hold of one of the necromancers standing beside him, putting a dagger to his throat. "We will set our ancestors free."

Meikah felt her magic rise, sending it to the dagger Hincke held, smiling when he let it go with a sound of pain. "I'm not about to let you complete your spell."

"Then you will die too." He raised his hands.

Not wanting to give him a chance to attack her, she attacked first, throwing lightning at him. Before she could attack again, the sounds of hoofbeats filled the area and assassins leapt from horses, attacking spirits and setting prisoners free. Meikah only took her gaze from Hincke for seconds, but when she looked back at him, he was fleeing on horseback. She took a step in his direction before common sense overrode anger and she returned to her companions, who still struggled with Daveth.

"Set him free," Maksim urged. "No one would want to be forced to serve an evil master against their will."

"No." The word burst from Meikah. "There has to be another way."

"Not unless you're willing to bind him to an object," Kellan said.

Meikah felt like she could hear the word 'too' hanging unspoken around them. "Hincke escaped. We need to figure out where he went."

"He'll probably be set free anyway," Maksim warned. "If the necromancer he's bound to loses his body, he'll go too, feeling the same painful death. It'll be less traumatic for him if you're the one who sets him free."

Meikah looked from Daveth to the direction Hincke had taken. "I can't kill him."

"He's already dead," Maksim said.

"Bind him," Marta pleaded. "Please bind him. He doesn't deserve this. Please, Meikah. Save him."

Chapter Twenty-Two

Meikah didn't know what to do. She wasn't sure she'd survived the first binding unscathed. What would a second one do to her? "We have to find Hincke." Maybe she could convince him to bind Daveth to an object in exchange for his life. His unnerving smile came to mind. And maybe she was coming up with desperate plans.

Marta yelped, glaring at Daveth as she drew back her hand. "He bit me."

"I know where he went." Daveth continued to struggle against them.

"Where?" Meikah asked.

"I've been commanded not to give aide to Hincke's enemies," Daveth said. "I want to tell you, but I can't form the words."

Meikah closed her eyes. They needed to find Hincke. He'd continue to capture people in an effort to set his grandfather free. If she did nothing, those a hundred and sixty-nine deaths would be on her conscience.

"No." Kellan said the word softly.

Meikah opened her eyes to meet his gaze. He was shaking his head.

"No, Meikah," Kellan begged. "I'll free him before I let you do that."

"I'll hold him," Marta offered, her gaze on Meikah.

"What are you planning?" Maksim asked.

Meikah wanted to tell them all to be quiet. That it was bad enough hearing the sounds of fighting in the background. She turned her back on Maksim and Kellan, facing Marta. She gave a slight nod at the question she could see in the warrior's eyes.

"No." Kellan let Daveth go.

Marta grabbed hold of Daveth before he could take more than a step.

"What are you doing, Meikah?" Maksim grabbed Meikah by the arm and turned her to face him.

She couldn't meet his gaze, dragging her arm from his grip. "What I need to."

"If Kellan thinks–" Maksim began.

Meikah interrupted him. "It's nothing I haven't done before." She drew her sword and grabbed hold of Daveth's hand. He tried to pull it away, causing a deeper cut on his palm than Meikah had planned. She let him go for a moment to allow it to heal slightly before grabbing his hand again and wrapping it around the pommel of the sword.

Like before, the words filled her mind and came easily. She didn't get far into the spell when her right hand burned, the heat swiftly filling her entire body. She met Marta's gaze as the silhouette of a dragon in flight darkened against the skin of her right hand and a lacey dragon burst into the sky.

Marta let go of Daveth, who'd stopped struggling a moment before the lacey dragon, that had grown in size, had settled over them. Before the wings of the dragon had blocked out her view, Meikah had caught a glimpse of Kellan holding Maksim back from her.

The heat increased and Meikah again thought she could smell burning flesh, the heat feeling worse than the previous time. The same mix of whitish-blue and fire-red lightning played across her skin as Daveth leaned into her, his forehead resting on hers as he cried out in pain, his other hand grabbing hold of her shoulder, his fingers digging in.

The pain from the heat and his grip caused her words to become laboured and she focused on speaking the last few, sinking to the ground when the dragon vanished in white light and red flames, Daveth sinking to the ground with her. This time when she would have let go of the pommel, Daveth released her shoulder and clamped her hand back over his.

He met her gaze. "Why did you never say how dangerous this was? How could Marta have let you risk yourself like this?"

Meikah smiled, a weary one that faded as soon as it had formed. "We need to find Hincke before he can kill again.

Not only a hundred and sixty-nine innocent people, but however many guards live at the necromancer prison."

Daveth's grip momentarily tightened on her hand. "I'll serve you for as long as you have need of me."

"I don't need that of you. As soon as I return home and can collect my other sword, this one will be yours," Meikah said.

"You have another weapon made of night steel?" Daveth asked.

She couldn't help smiling at the shock in his tone. "No. It's a normal blade."

"Then I can't take this one until you can replace it with the same. I'll remain at your side until that's done," Daveth promised.

"That isn't ne-"

Maksim knelt beside them, reaching for her only to lower his hand. "Meikah? Are you unharmed?"

She drew back from Daveth, automatically taking her sword when he pressed it into her hand. "We need to find Hincke." She tried to rise to her feet, needing to take the hand Kellan held out.

He kept hold of her when she tried to pull away. "You're burning up again."

"It's the dragon burning away that which would harm her," Marta said.

Meikah stared at Marta. "Harm me?"

Marta nodded.

"My necromancer abilities?"

Marta shrugged. "No dragon touched was ever a necromancer back when I lived."

"Does that mean she can do necromancer spells without becoming one?" Kellan asked.

Again Marta shrugged. "Who knows how much the dragon can protect her from. It's not all powerful. Eventually it will fail and harm will win."

Meikah's gaze was drawn to the faint silhouette of a dragon in flight on her right hand. It wasn't as dark as it normally was, but then usually it was either there and plain to see or invisible. She didn't have time to figure it out. She turned to Daveth. "You said you know where Hincke went."

"When he was getting ready, he talked to one of the necromancers he seemed to be on good terms with. He said he'd meet him at the cave if anything went wrong. That he's been taking supplies there every morning on his way to meet him at the northern village, to add to what they'd stored there. Supplies small enough no one would miss them or notice him taking them. From what I could work out, the direction seemed to be the same as that of the cave Marta and I stayed in on our way to Port Mayren all those years ago," Daveth said.

"I remember the cave," Marta said. "You were surprised to learn how close we were to Port Mayren and wished we'd kept travelling so we could have been in a warm bed rather than be stuck using the bedroll that had become damp in the rain."

Daveth nodded. "I'm fairly certain I can locate it." A wry smile formed. "Like it was only last week."

Marta laughed softly. "Memories of our life do seem stronger than those from the time after our death." She glanced over her shoulder. "Did you want me to collect the horses?"

"We'll all go," Kellan said.

Meikah followed Kellan, keeping her gaze on his back rather than look in Maksim's direction. She couldn't meet Maksim's gaze. Not with how worried he'd looked. What would he say when they were alone? Would he fear her? Would he be disgusted that she'd used a necromancer's spell? Not once, but twice.

"We'll be a horse short." Marta glanced at Daveth before looking at Meikah. "I can travel in the dagger if you wish."

Meikah shook her head. "Daveth can ride with me." It was probably best they were all available in case they ran into any of the fighting she could hear come from different directions throughout the forest.

Reaching the horses, they mounted and headed in the direction Daveth indicated. They hadn't ridden far when four necromancers came towards them, also mounted.

"Ride on," Maksim ordered. "I'll slow them down and bait them towards some of the fighting still going on."

"You can't face them alone," Meikah protested.

"I'll stay with him," Marta offered. "You don't need both me and Daveth to help you find the cave."

"Go, Meikah." Maksim rode towards the necromancers, leaning over the neck of his horse when one of them sent a gust of air towards him.

Marta took the dagger Meikah held out to her before riding after Maksim, leaping from her horse as she drew near.

"That way." Daveth tugged on the reins of the horse, turning her head slightly.

Chapter Twenty-Three

Meikah was half tempted to ask Daveth if he'd prefer her to sit behind him, but she liked seeing where they were going too much. She also liked seeing what was ahead of them and what they might face.

Twenty minutes later, Daveth slowed the horse. "Everything looks so different."

"Did you expect it to stay the same after all these years?" Kellan asked.

"No, but…" Daveth's voice trailed off and he sighed. "I don't suppose you have a map."

Kellan brought his horse to a stop, dismounting and taking out the map. He unfolded it and held it for Daveth, who'd also dismounted. "The circled mark is where Hincke planned to kill everyone."

Daveth glanced around, running his finger across the map when he focused on it again. He glanced around again before shifting his finger across slightly. "I think we need to go further over this way." He shifted his finger across some more.

"Are you certain?" Kellan folded the map when Daveth lowered his hand.

"Not completely." Daveth turned to Meikah. "I'm sorry. I should have realised that even the landmarks would have changed. That people would move boulders to either use them or build where they were, that some of them might become overgrown and lost in the undergrowth and trees are felled or grow. That even roads might fall into disuse and new ones be created."

"You've given us an area to look in," Meikah said. It was more than what they'd previously had.

Daveth swung up behind Meikah. "There are spells that would allow you to track him."

"Not without something of his," Meikah said.

"I wasn't talking about sorcerer spells."

"No." She was still burning up and didn't dare risk using another necromancer spell while the dragon fought against the harm from binding Daveth to her sword.

"After all you've done to try and find him, I felt it worth pointing out," Daveth said.

"Only as a last resort. We'll see if we can find him by searching first." She'd have to be extremely desperate to try another necromancer spell while she burned as much as she did.

They rode around for what felt like hours, but judging by the glimpses Meikah caught of the moon, it hadn't shifted enough for that much time to have passed. A few times Daveth dismounted to check in overgrown areas, shaking his head each time before mounting behind Meikah again.

"Should we-" Meikah broke off as she caught a scent. "Is that food cooking or am I imagining things?"

"If you are, I am too," Kellan said.

"It might be a traveller camped up along the side of one of the dirt tracks cutting through the forest," Daveth warned.

"If it is, I suggest we beg them for something to eat." Kellan grinned. "It's been hours since we've eaten. Although I don't know why someone would cook this late at night."

Meikah turned her horse in the direction of the scent of cooking, dismounting along with Daveth and Kellan and walking as the scent grew stronger. They tied their horses to some trees before continuing. The flicker of a campfire highlighted the edges of a cave once they were close enough.

"This is it," Daveth whispered. "This is the cave we stayed in. There's a narrow exit at the other end. Marta discovered it."

"How deep is the cave?" Kellan asked.

"Deep enough that those two by the fire might not be the only ones here." Daveth nodded towards Hincke and his companion, who sat on wooden stools, talking too quietly for them to hear what was said.

"Is it easy to find the exit?" Kellan asked.

"At first glance it looks like a crack running down the rock," Daveth said. "I can make sure they don't escape that way."

"You wouldn't last long against necromancers," Kellan said. "I'll see if I can find it."

Meikah turned to Daveth. "Go with Kellan. Show him where it is."

"Who will protect you?" Daveth asked. "I'd stay here and fight at your side if I could. But that's impossible since you've ordered me away."

"If you want, you can come back after Kellan finds the cave." She hadn't realised it had been an order he couldn't ignore. "I wasn't ordering you. It just made sense that you show him."

Daveth studied her for a moment. "It's going to take time becoming accustomed to being at someone's beck and call. Even when I served dragons, I was never compelled to do their bidding. I chose to do it."

"Can we sort this out later?" Kellan asked. "I want to attack while we have the advantage. While these two are unaware we're here and before they're joined by anyone else."

Daveth inclined his head, leading the way off to the right, Kellan following him.

Meikah watched them go, regularly glancing at the two necromancers by the fire. The other man rose to check on the food, nodding as he tasted it. Hincke also rose, but instead of moving closer to the fire, he turned to go further into the cave. Not sure if that would put Kellan and Daveth in danger, she stepped out from her hiding place.

"Hincke! Surrender while you can." She moved forward as she spoke, stopping several feet away from the fire.

Hincke spun to face her, laughing. "Do you really think you're going to fight the two of us?"

"I stopped you from killing all those innocent people, didn't I?" Meikah asked.

Hincke's laughter faded. "It won't matter. I'll find more. Now I don't have to worry about remaining unnoticed, I can collect them as quickly as I want."

"The King will send patrols throughout the forest until they find you." She didn't know if he would, but it sounded likely. "It'll be impossible for you to find another hundred and sixty-nine people when so many are searching for you." She only wished it was true.

Both Hincke and his companion laughed. It was his companion who spoke this time. "I think we should capture this one and make her the first one of our next hundred and sixty-nine."

Hincke shook his head. "I say we use her to create a spell of confusion to turn away all those who come close to the cave."

"What about the ones we told to meet up here if things went wrong? All the group leaders," Hincke's companion said.

Hincke glared at his companion for a moment. "I suppose we better hold off on casting that spell until they're here." He glanced past Meikah. "Or until the sun rises. Any that aren't here by then likely aren't coming. We can't wait around for them forever."

Meikah had to keep her hand still when she heard others were to meet them at the cave. She'd been tempted to draw her sword and attack before their reinforcements arrived. "All the necromancers were looking rather outnumbered when we left. I doubt any will turn up. How many were you expecting?"

"As if I'd give you any information," Hincke said.

"Oh, only a couple then." Meikah smiled at him. "You want me to think there are more coming than are actually on their way. That's if any of them escape."

Hincke's companion looked her up and down before turning to Hincke. "She's not very good at this, is she?"

Hincke's lips pressed tightly together as he looked Meikah over. "I wouldn't let her youth and seeming ineptitude fool you. She's more cunning than you think."

Chapter Twenty-Four

Meikah somehow managed not to laugh at Hincke's comment. She wasn't at all cunning. She was struggling to think of ways to keep them distracted and learn information. She had only managed to do the first.

Daveth stepped out from behind some trees, closer to the cave entrance and off to her right. Both the necromancers noticed him instantly.

"Maybe we should ask how many will be joining you here." Hincke's companion drew his sword a few seconds before Hincke drew his.

"I told you she was cunning," Hincke said. "This was obviously a ploy to wait for help." His eyes narrowed. "That's one of the spirits from Durnning Island. You're a necromancer, not a sorcerer." He glared at Meikah. "Was anything you told me the truth?"

Not bothering to answer his question, Meikah drew her sword, wishing she had her dagger with her. She only hoped Daveth's arrival meant Kellan was in place.

"Well?" Hincke demanded.

Kellan came into view behind the two necromancers. "She isn't the only one who wants to stop the two of you from setting your ancestors free."

Hincke turned so he could keep the three of them in sight. "You're a necromancer too?"

Kellan grinned. "I'm whatever I feel like being at the time." Mist formed behind him, spreading out and enveloping him. "Should we see what I currently feel like being?" He attacked Hincke's companion, his movements hard to follow due to the mist that hung around his body and at times cloaked him.

Worried Hincke might also attack Kellan, Meikah cast lightning at the ground near his feet. A shiver went through her when Hincke faced her with a smile before striding towards her. The smile was pure evil.

"If you can't bring yourself to attack to kill, you have no chance of winning this battle." Hincke attacked her as he spoke the last word.

"I have no problem causing a death." Daveth joined Meikah, a broken branch in his hands.

Hincke laughed. "A spirit can do very little against a necromancer."

Meikah blocked Hincke's attack. "But what can a spirit and a necromancer do against another necromancer?"

"So you are a necromancer?" Hincke drove Meikah back with a flurry of attacks, barely pausing in them to block Daveth's slower ones.

Meikah couldn't very well deny it anymore. Not after having done two necromancer spells. But that wasn't all she was. A smile formed as she shifted her sword to her left hand. "I'm dragon touched." And somehow or other, she managed to make the lacey dragon attack Hincke on demand. A larger, brighter one, this one like green lightning, attacked at the same time.

Hincke stumbled back, both hands on his sword as he blocked the lacey dragons. "Then who is the necromancer?" He tried to go on the offensive, but Daveth swung the branch at him.

Instead of answering, Meikah tried to again attack with her dragon. This time it took two attempts, but since Hincke was already off balance from Daveth's attack, the few extra seconds didn't matter. She kept up her attacks on Hincke, determined to subdue him before any of his people could arrive to help.

"I think whatever you are, you don't know much about it at all." The only warning they had was Hincke's lips curving into his unnerving smile.

Daveth was flung back, colliding with a tree, his lacey dragon splintering into sparks of light that scattered and faded. He slumped against the ground, trying to push himself upright.

Meikah stepped between Hincke and Daveth, blocking the next attack, one which was meant for the warrior. "And why would you say that?"

"Because those pauses aren't hesitations about harming me, they're you trying to use your skills." Hincke smiled at her. "Or what you have in the way of skills."

Meikah found herself struggling to block his next flurry of attacks. She had no chance to help Daveth rise or check to see if Kellan was faring any better than the two of them. She obviously needed far more training. Had Tolmerr been correct? Should she have remained behind to let those who were more skilled take care of things?

"Did you really think I was so inexperienced that I wouldn't have plans in place for times like this?" Hincke took five knuckle bones out of a pocket and threw them on the ground. With a few muttered words, they became armed skeletons.

Meikah backed away as the skeletons advanced. The only good thing was that the five of them had swords and shields. If one of the skeletons had been using a bow, she would have been in worse trouble. Not that she knew how she'd defeat five skeletons and a necromancer.

Hincke turned away, striding towards his horse as he sheathed his sword. The two horses had remained calmly grazing after an initial glance in the direction of the fight.

Meikah looked between the skeletons and Hincke. There was no way she could get past them and prevent him from escaping. Yet again. She tightened her grip on her sword. After all the effort it had taken to find him, he was about to get away again.

Daveth finally rose to his feet, once again holding the broken branch. He took several steps towards Hincke, glancing at Meikah who continued to retreat from the skeletons.

It was a pity she didn't have Rafe's ability to throw fireballs so she could cremate the bones. She thought wistfully of the vampire who'd remained in Dreyton. There was a chance he and Amiel might not be the only dead staying at Fable with how things were going. "Don't worry about me," she told Daveth. "Stop Hincke."

At Meikah's words, Hincke turned to face them, his gaze drawn to Daveth. "Are you hoping to make your death permanent, spirit?"

"Not any time soon." Daveth cast his dragon at the two horses, the lacey apparition cutting through the reins and scaring them off.

Drawing his sword, Hincke again smiled unnervingly. "Do you think that's my only way of getting away from here?" Before he attacked, he took a bone from a different pocket and threw it on the ground. His sword slashed past the broken branch, missing Daveth by inches. Behind him, a skeletal horse grew from the bone that had been flung on the ground. It tossed its head, snorting.

Meikah darted in and attacked the skeleton on the left, wondering how one cared for a horse like the one Hincke had summoned. Did they need to eat? Or did dead creatures have no need for sustenance the same as dead people? She jumped back out of the way when the skeletons tried to surround her. Things were not looking good. And unlike Hincke, they weren't expecting reinforcements.

The skeletons kept coming for her. Their movements slow, but relentless. Their focus completely on her. Backing away, she cast lightning at them. The one it struck stumbled backwards before continuing to come after her. Grinning when she actually managed to slow one, even if it was only for a few seconds, Meikah focused on using her lightning. She wanted to check on Daveth and Kellan, but she didn't have time. Not if she wanted to deal with the skeletons before they had the chance to surround her. All she knew was that her two companions still fought, the sounds of them fighting punctuating the night.

Chapter Twenty-Five

Backing away further, Meikah noticed the ground beneath the skeletons filled with puddles. Before the skeletons could step past them, she cast lightning at the ground, shielding her eyes from the flare of light. A grin escaped when she saw the charred remains of the skeletons, their weapons scattered across the ground. The last of the lightning that played across the puddles winked out and she darted forward, grabbing one of the swords. "Daveth." When he glanced in her direction, she held up the sword. At his nod, she tossed it to him.

He dropped the branch and grabbed the sword, his attention on Hincke. "Toss me a second one."

Meikah grabbed another sword and waited until he glanced in her direction, after blocking Hincke's attack, before she tossed it towards him. Stepping around the skeleton remains, she strode towards Hincke with a glance at Kellan. He appeared to be holding his own against Hincke's companion, who didn't seem to have any of Hincke's tricks ready to use.

Daveth attacked with a flurry of movements, blocking each of Hincke's attacks. Even though he held a sword in each hand, he was regularly able to attack with his dragon.

Meikah joined Daveth, the two of them driving Hincke backwards. "Not doing so well now, are you?" She filled his sword with lightning, grinning when he dropped it with a curse.

"It doesn't matter if you capture me or kill me. There are others who'll carry on my work of freeing those necromancers who were wrongly imprisoned. As long as we're treated this way, we'll fight for survival. We'll fight to be treated fairly and show those who've persecuted us what it's like to be the ones persecuted. Necromancers shouldn't be sent from their homes and families all because of something they can't help. This is our country too."

Kellan joined them, turning the ground beneath Hincke's feet muddy so he slipped. "We might be born with the skills to be necromancers, but we can choose not to use them. Choose to be something better than what using those spells makes us."

Hincke tried to keep his balance. He went down, Daveth pinning him to the ground before he could rise. He looked past Daveth, meeting Meikah's gaze when she moved closer. "You haven't won."

Kellan grinned. "Looks like we have to me." He strode into the cave, glancing over his shoulder before entering.

"I'll grab more of the rope I used to tie up the other necromancer."

His words made Meikah look at Hincke's companion. He was tied at both the hands and feet as well as gagged. He lay on his back, but his head was turned in their direction. From the glare he gave them and the anger in his eyes, he'd make them pay for all they'd done. That was if he could escape.

It didn't take them long to tie Hincke and gag him so they didn't have to keep listening to him talk about how they'd regret their part in his capture. Kellan put out the fire, helping himself to the food as they made certain there were no coals that might catch the forest on fire. Daveth watched the two necromancers, both swords in his hands as he stood guard, regularly scanning the area.

Meikah put the swords and shields in the cave rather than leave them lying about, surveying the primitive set up. It was basic with several bedrolls stacked along one wall, a table near them and a few closed chests that she soon discovered contained preserved food, cookware and utensils. It would have been sufficient to keep him hidden for a few weeks until everyone gave up looking for him. Returning outside, it was to find Kellan and Daveth discussing how to get the two prisoners back to Port Mayren.

Kellan shook his head. "You can't ride the skeleton horse and we can't take the time to search for the horses you chased away."

"I'll walk beside you and they can go on the back of each of your horses with you," Daveth offered.

"You could return to the sword," Kellan suggested.

"And what about my new swords?" Daveth asked. "What will happen to them?"

"They'd be left behind since you don't have a sheath for them," Kellan said.

As much as Meikah wanted Daveth to remain with them since they didn't know what else was in the forest, it was too far for him to walk to Port Mayren. Even being a spirit and not in need of sleep and sustenance he could still be fatigued and need rest. "I can tear apart a sheet from one of the bedrolls in the cave and bundle up the swords so I can take them to Port Mayren. We'll find a way to get you two sheathes." She wasn't sure how, since she had very little money of her own.

"When we leave Port Mayren and return home, we'll see about getting you better weapons." Kellan picked up Hincke's companion and slung him over the back of his horse.

While Kellan dealt with their prisoners, she returned inside the cave and tore up one of the sheets for a length of cloth to wrap the swords in. She then used another length to bind them crosswise on her back out of the way. With one more look around the area, she mounted her horse, hating the idea of having Hincke behind her.

Daveth stood beside her. "If there's trouble, call me out to fight."

She nodded.

"Might be better to leave him in the sword and see if having a more powerful weapon helps," Kellan suggested.

Daveth rested his hand on the pommel of Meikah's sheathed sword. "Don't leave me in the sword forever."

She met his gaze, seeing the worry in his eyes. "I won't." When the worry remained, she added, "I promise."

With a nod, he vanished, the sword momentarily heating.

The flare of heat in her sword made Meikah realise she was no longer overheated from the last necromancer spell she'd performed. Either it hadn't been as dangerous as the first time or her dragon touched abilities were getting better at protecting her. Having no idea, she made a mental note to ask one of the dragon touched warriors later and turned towards Kellan. "What are we going to do with the horse?" She nodded towards the skeleton horse.

He studied it. "I guess we can't leave it here. Anyone might find it." He gathered up the reins. "At least we'll be able to point out it belongs to the necromancers we captured. Otherwise, the citizens of Port Mayren might run us out with pitchforks and lit torches."

Meikah couldn't return his grin. His description was too accurate. When he started towards the capital, she urged her horse to come alongside his, remaining silent.

There was nothing she wanted to talk about while Hincke and his companion were listening.

They were over three quarters of the way back to the capital and Meikah was beginning to think it'd be an uneventful journey when four necromancers on horseback caught up with them. Meikah recognised one of them. It was the necromancer Hincke had planned to kill. For a second she hoped he was coming to return the favour to Hincke.

"Release them," the necromancer demanded, riding alongside them.

Meikah slowed her horse, letting it come to a stop so she could easily dismount if the necromancers attacked. She wasn't that skilled at fighting from horseback. "Hincke was going to kill you."

"We've all pledged our lives to the cause," the necromancer said.

"Has Hincke?" Kellan asked.

"We need leaders to carry us to victory," one of the other necromancers said.

"To carry you to victory or to convert you to his way of thinking?" Kellan asked.

One of the other necromancers drew her sword. "We won't ask again. Release them or we'll set them free through force."

Meikah didn't like their chances of winning against four necromancers. "Give us a minute to discuss it."

"Do you think us idiots?" one of the necromancers demanded. "All you'll do is take time to plan your next move."

"Five minutes. That's not enough time to plan anything," Meikah said.

"You can have two minutes," the necromancer who'd remained silent until now, said. The other three argued with him.

Not about to waste the chance to plan at least something, Meikah rode close to Kellan, leaning towards him and keeping her voice low, glad the skeleton horse was on the other side of him out of the way. "You ride to the capital. We can't risk Hincke escaping. Daveth and I will keep them from following. I have an idea." She wasn't sure if it was a good one, but it should at least give Kellan a head start.

"I'm not leaving you here to face them on your own," Kellan protested.

"We don't have time to argue. You can be there in less than twenty minutes. Come back for me and bring help." Meikah handed over the reins of her horse, dismounting and taking several steps towards the necromancers. "We've come to a decision."

"He's leaving." The woman pointed at Kellan, taking a step forward.

Chapter Twenty-Six

Guessing she no longer needed to tell them their answer, Meikah threw lightning at them, casting it around the group so they were caged by it. Drawing her sword in preparation for when she could no longer keep up the ring of lightning, streaks of it sparking off in different directions out of control, she braced herself for their attack. Fireballs came through the gaps in the ring of lightning and she dodged to the side, one section of the lightning ring going down for a few seconds. She had it up again before any of them could escape, two of them having to jump back out of the way.

Before Meikah could release Daveth from the sword, one of the necromancers formed a shield, exploding it outwards and taking out her ring of lightning. The four necromancers advanced on her, one of them throwing fireballs as he did, a sword in one hand.

Meikah blocked one of the fireballs with her sword, the metal heating and filling with her magic in response. Lightning flickered along the blade, quickly joined by a green lacey dragon that wound its way along the metal, the lightning playing across its body. Shocked by its appearance, Meikah missed blocking the oncoming fireball. The dragon spread its wings, the size increasing rapidly to deflect the attack before shrinking back to its original size.

The necromancers halted, the four of them sharing a look with each other. It was the woman who spoke. "You've bound a dragon to your sword? You don't look old enough to have the power to do so difficult a spell."

Meikah smiled, not about to tell them it was a dragon touched warrior. "Is it really? I hadn't noticed. The spell seemed easy enough to me." How long could she keep them distracted? Long enough for Kellan to reach Port Mayren and return to help her? It could take him an hour by the time he handed their prisoners over.

"You're from the Arcton Mountains?" one of the necromancers asked.

"I've been there." She kept her smile in place, not about to tell them the name of her hometown. Dreyton didn't need any more trouble turning up. Not after getting rid of the Society Against Vampires.

"Join us." The woman gestured towards Meikah's sword. "Having a weapon like that guarantees the King will hunt you down once he learns of it."

Meikah pushed aside the fears the words made flare. Should she explain what she'd done to the King? Would he be better off not knowing? She kept her smile in place, refusing to let them see how much the words had bothered her. How long had it been since Kellan had left? It felt like ages, but she doubted it had been more than ten minutes. "I really don't think any of you are in a position to tell him and I'm not about to go running to the King and show him what I've done." Although it was a possibility she'd tell him rather than let him hear about it from someone else.

"We can protect you. We're working to make this country a safer place for those like us," the woman said.

"Why would you invite me to join you when I've sent your leader to the King?" Meikah wasn't sure it was a good question to ask, but she was struggling to think of ways to keep the conversation going so they didn't attack again. An hour was beginning to seem like a really long time. There was no way she could keep them talking that long.

One of the men shrugged. "We have other leaders. Hincke is one of the best planners, but he isn't the only one capable of leading us to victory."

Her heart sank at learning they hadn't prevented anything. She tried to think of what to do next. "What do you plan to do if you win?"

One of the men laughed. "We will win. It's only a matter of time and we certainly have plenty of that on our side." His companions laughed with him, the woman nodding instead of laughing.

The woman took a step towards Meikah. "You could do better than hiding who you really are. Don't you want to be yourself? Have people accept you for who you are? Be amongst your own kind?"

Was this how Hincke had gained such a big following? It certainly hadn't been from his unnerving smile. "How do I know what you offer is any better than what I already have?"

Kellan stepped out from behind a tree. "Is that offer only open to one of us, or both?"

Meikah stared at him, wanting to demand what he'd done with Hincke and his companion. As well as the horses. He hadn't had the time to reach Port Mayren then return here.

"Where is Hincke?" one of the necromancers asked.

"I handed him and his friend over to a patrol of the King's men to take back to Port Mayren." Kellan shrugged. "It was the job we were paid to do."

"That's all this was to you?" one of the necromancers demanded. "A job?"

Kellan nodded. "We need to eat. Not like there are many jobs on offer where they don't care who you are."

"The offer is available to both of you," the woman said. "But only if she accepts." She nodded towards Meikah while keeping her gaze on Kellan.

"What's so special about her?" Kellan asked.

"The dragon bound to her blade," the woman said.

Kellan looked from Meikah to the blade she held before turning his attention back to the woman. "How do you know that?"

"We saw the dragon when she attacked," the woman said.

"Why are we even bothering with them, Naya?" the necromancer Hinkce had planned to kill demanded. "We have more important things to do than worry about a couple of children."

Naya gave him a look that had him taking several steps back. "I will say what we worry about." When he didn't reply, she demanded, "Understand?"

He nodded, taking another step back. "Perfectly." He sent a glare in Meikah's direction.

"When do we need to give you an answer?" Kellan asked.

"They just want to talk about it so they can come up with another plan against us," the same necromancer said.

Kellan grinned. "Not at all what I'm trying to do. I'm not about to take your offer if there's a better one. Who knows what job we'll be offered when we return to Port Mayren to collect our payment."

Meikah somehow managed not to laugh at the way Kellan was acting. He seemed to be enjoying himself a little too much. Although she shouldn't be surprised since he was busy making plans that would probably lead to trouble. A lot of trouble.

"Is that all that matters to you?" Naya demanded. "Don't you want more than you currently have?"

"Of course I do," Kellan said. "But that usually involves money. Lots of it."

"I don't think they're right for our organisation," the same necromancer said.

Naya turned on him with a sharp look. "Did I ask for your opinion, Ervass?"

"No," Ervass muttered, again sending a glare in Meikah's direction.

She wanted to demand what she'd done wrong. It had been Kellan who'd mentioned money. Not her.

Naya turned back to face Meikah. "I can give you until this evening. We'll leave a message here to tell you where to find us. And don't go thinking you'll be able to set a trap. We'll send a spirit with the message. At midnight."

"That'll give us enough time to decide," Kellan said. "Nearly a full day."

Naya kept her gaze on Meikah. "I want your answer, not his. What do you say?"

"What if we decide we don't like your organisation?" Meikah asked.

"Oh, you'll like it."

Chapter Twenty-Seven

Meikah shivered when Naya smiled at her. It was worse than any of Hincke's smiles. This one warned her she'd like it or die. Forcing herself to return the smile, Meikah nodded. "At midnight." She stayed in the middle of the road, watching as the four necromancers left, still holding her sword, unwilling to sheath it until she knew they were far enough away they couldn't attack her or Kellan.

Kellan came to stand beside her. "You want to tell me everything they said? I didn't manage to hear all of it. Only enough to know we need to find the rest of them."

Meikah briefly told him, sheathing her sword as she did. She glanced in the direction of Port Mayren. "Did you really come across a patrol?"

Kellan nodded. "They had a couple of prisoners with them, so they didn't mind another two. Especially when I told them who Hincke was. They were also fascinated by the skeleton horse." He took a step towards the forest. "I left our horses back a bit so I could sneak up and have the advantage."

Meikah followed him through the forest. "What are we going to do about Naya's offer?"

"We need to take it. How else are we going to find out where the rest of them are?" Reaching the horses, Kellan untied the reins of his from a branch. "But we can't tell the King or Tolmerr. They'd only get in the way and send others instead. The only way Naya would accept them instead of you is if they had your sword and claimed it as their own. I doubt Daveth would appreciate that."

Meikah, who'd just mounted her horse, stared at him. "That's crazy. What happens if something goes wrong? We can't go alone." Yet there was no way she'd give her sword to someone who'd probably never let Daveth leave it. He didn't deserve to become someone's slave.

"If we took too many with us, they'd be suspicious." Kellan turned his horse towards the capital. "It'll have to be only the two of us."

"I don't know." Meikah rode alongside him the moment they returned to the road, trying to think of what else they could do. She slowly shook her head. "It sounds like a terrible idea." But she could think of no other to replace it.

Kellan grinned. "All the best ones usually sound that way."

"How can that make them the best?" Meikah asked.

"They're the ones that get results."

Meikah sighed. She did want results. She wanted all of Hincke's necromancers caught and imprisoned so they couldn't set their ancestors free. Their ancestors who'd nearly been successful in overthrowing the King's grandfather. A shiver ran through her. They couldn't let them be freed. That sounded like a worse idea than Kellan's plan.

By the time they reached Port Mayren, Meikah still had no idea what to do. Reaching Garven's home, she let Shade take her horse and set Daveth free from the sword, giving him the swords she'd brought back with her.

Isha met them at the door, Marta with her. She wrapped her arms around Meikah. "I was worried about you. Especially when everyone else returned and you didn't."

"I'm safe." She returned Isha's hug, trying not to think about the decision she had to make. Going with Naya wouldn't be in the least bit safe.

Isha released her, stepping back so she could enter the house. "Tolmerr sent word that you're to report to him when you arrive."

Dread pooled in her stomach. Would he kick her out of the Assassins Of The Dead? What would she do then? Permanently joining Naya wasn't an option. She'd rather live in the Arcton Mountains.

Kellan followed them inside. "We'll see him after we've seen the King. Did he leave a messenger here to escort us back?"

Isha nodded. "He's in the kitchen having a bite to eat. His eyes lit up when I said the housekeeper was making spicy fruit pastries."

Meikah laughed when Kellan's expression brightened at the words. "Sounds like you want some too."

"Think you can sneak a couple out of there for us before we see the King?" Kellan asked Isha.

Shade came towards them from inside the house. "No need. I swiped a few on my way through. The messenger asked if you were back yet. Told him I'd go check." He handed a pastry to each of them. "Ready to see the King?"

Meikah wanted to decline, wishing she could sleep since it was now sometime during the very early hours of the morning. Instead, she nodded, her mouth full of warm spicy fruit and flaky pastry. Going to see the King had to be preferable to seeing Tolmerr. Especially after disobeying him.

Kellan turned to Isha. "Give us five minutes and then let the messenger know we had to see the King and will call on Tolmerr on our way back."

Swallowing her mouthful, Meikah looked from Marta to Daveth. "The two of you can come with us this time." She needed to talk to them about letting the King know what she'd done. Before he found out from someone else.

As soon as they were far enough from the house, and had eaten their pastries, Kellan told Shade all that had happened, the three of them walking slowly so they had enough time to discuss everything.

"You need to accept their offer," Shade said. "It's important we find out who the leaders are, where they're hiding and what they're planning."

Meikah sighed. "After how many times Hincke escaped, I'm not sure we're up to the task. Or at least I'm not."

"We'll help," Marta offered. "We were trained as warriors. We can fight alongside you."

"They could carry messages to Shade," Kellan suggested. "They could slip in and out unnoticed from wherever we're staying."

"That's another thing," Meikah said. "I need to tell the King what I've done. Before someone else lets him know I've bound spirits to my weapons." She argued it back and forth with Kellan when he protested.

Shade finally interrupted. "Meikah's right. If the King learns of it from someone else, it'll go worse for her. She's not the typical necromancer. As long as we can prove she hasn't changed, he'll accept what she's done and protect her from others who might not accept it."

"He'll only protect her as long as it's of benefit to him," Kellan said.

"Then we make sure she remains important and continues to be beneficial to the country," Shade said.

Meikah wanted to protest, but she lost the chance when Marta and Daveth started planning ways to prove to the King that she was the same person. That the dragon had protected her from being harmed while doing the spells.

They made their way to the same entrance they always used, relieved one of the usual guards was on duty, a different one with him. He sent the other guard to find out if the King would see her while he eyed her companions up and down.

Meikah remained silent, even though she could see the guard had questions he wished he could ask. She supposed not having an exact idea of what she was to the King helped to keep him silent rather than interrogate her.

The other guard returned. "The King will see you now." He led the way through numerous corridors, lightly tapping on a door and opening it when the King called out his permission.

Meikah glanced around the room, taking in the filled bookcases, the desk in the corner and the fireplace ready to be lit, her gaze coming to a rest on the King who was in an armchair by the fireplace.

The King set aside the letter he was reading, closing it before putting it on the small, decorative table beside his armchair. "I was informed I have you to thank for capturing Hincke, the leader of the attack on my prison."

Chapter Twenty-Eight

Meikah started to say Hincke was only one of the leaders, but Kellan spoke first.

"We were happy to help, Your Highness." He bowed. "But some of his people escaped, so there's the possibility they'll try and rescue him or break into the prison without his help."

"We're relocating the prisoners and dividing them between several hidden, underground prisons so we don't risk all of them being freed at the same time again. We're also leaving the one who can be tracked at the original prison and putting Hincke and his companions in a prison that contains only them in case one of them can be tracked," the King said. "Unless you have any ideas to improve the plans."

Kellan shook his head. "None that I can think of."

"There's a spell that could remove any spells on them, including tracking spells," Shade said. "But it's a necromancer spell."

"I won't allow human sacrifice," the King said.

"It doesn't have to be a human for this particular spell," Shade explained.

The King hesitated, then shook his head. "There are no necromancers I'd trust."

Meikah took a deep breath. "Then maybe what I have to tell you will help." She urged Marta and Daveth forward. "These two spirits are dragon touched."

"Spirits?" The King studied them. "How is it I can see them?"

Meikah began to reach for her sword, lowering her hand before she touched it. "Can I draw my sword?"

The King gave her a nod.

She took out the sword, holding it out to him. "Daveth is bound to this weapon. He had information we needed to catch Hincke and I can use necromancer spells without them effecting me because I'm dragon touched."

Branok took the sword from her. "I've heard of weapons created this way, centuries ago. Powerful weapons."

"I've promised Daveth the sword belongs to him while he's bound to it." Meikah kept her tone even and calm when she would have preferred demanding Branok return the ssword and not even think about using it for himself.

"How does being dragon touched protect you?" Branok held the sword out.

Meikah took the sword, trying not to show how relieved she was at having it returned.

Marta grinned. "I can show you how being dragon touched protects her if you let me draw a weapon." She gestured to the dagger at her side.

Again Branok gave a nod.

Marta stepped behind Daveth and stabbed at him with the dagger, a lacey dragon rising from his hand to block her attack. She tried again. The dragon once more prevented her. She took a step to the side, giving a nod to Daveth before turning to the King. "When we're about to be harmed without our knowledge or when we're unable to fight back against harm, the dragon fights for us."

"It's separate to you?" Branok asked.

Marta sheathed the dagger. "No, it's part of us. A part of our inner self. A part that's always aware of what's going on around us and has become draconic through the changes the dragon caused in us."

"Dragon touched are no longer human?" Branok asked.

Marta shook her head. "No, we're human. A small part of us is altered, like a shield that is always with us."

"It's like we've been given a shell to protect us, like the turtle has one. It's us made a little different so it can be of better use to us," Daveth said. "A way of protecting us, bestowed upon us by a dragon so we can face the dangers involved in helping dragons."

"What type of dangers?" Branok asked.

Daveth's smile was filled with sorrow. "I couldn't tell you what dangers dragon touched would face these days." He glanced at Meikah. "But I can assure you that the dragon part of Meikah has kept her safe from the necromancer spells she's used."

"How many spells have you used?" Branok asked Meikah.

"Only the two."

"So you can't be certain it will always work," Branok said.

"We can be certain," Daveth said. "It's the way of dragon touched. Now if she did spell after spell and didn't give the dragon time to recover, that would be different."

"How is it you can tell if the dragon has recovered?" Branok asked.

Meikah held out her right hand. "There's no faint shadow of a dragon on my hand."

Branok took hold of her hand and examined it before he let go. "What would you need to do this spell?"

"Five small animals. Rats, birds or any type of similar sized pest that you would be rid of," Shade said. "And four bottles of wine. The spell is strong enough to cast on four bottles, but you'll need only a single drop for each necromancer, so hopefully there'll be enough. If not, I'm sure Meikah could do it again another day."

"One drop." Branok sounded sceptical.

Shade nodded. "A single drop of wine on the tongue is the easiest way to administer it. The wine will sink in without them needing to swallow it."

"I'll see that it's arranged," Branok said. "Can I witness the spell or will it harm me?"

"It won't harm you." Shade turned to Meikah. "The decision is up to you."

"I don't know the spell," Meikah said.

"I'll write it down for you." Shade smiled. "Then burn it once it's read."

Meikah nodded, turning to Branok. "You can witness." It seemed the best way to reassure the King. "But we were meant to see Tolmerr today. Could you send someone to let him know we're here at your request?"

"It'll be done." Branok summoned a servant and things were quickly arranged. Five rodents that had been caught in the dungeons were brought in along with four bottles of wine, parchment, pen and ink.

As soon as Meikah had learned the spell Shade had written out, he lit a fire in the fireplace, using his ability with wind to help the flames catch more quickly. Once it was burning brightly, he tossed the parchment in, the paper curling in on itself as flames took hold.

Branok chuckled. "That ability could come in handy."

Shade gave a single nod, smiling in agreement before stepping back out of the way so Meikah could perform the spell.

She thought she'd be bothered by how many watched. Especially since one of them was the King. Yet the moment she started to recite the spell, it was like her body knew all the actions she needed to perform and went straight to work. She was relieved the spell called for a sacrifice and not a painful death, swiftly ending the lives of the rodents. As she smeared the blood from them on the bottles of wine, reciting the last of the spell, the dragon burst forth, enveloping her as she stepped back from the bottles, the spell done.

The heat in her body increased, but not to the same extent as it had with her last two spells. Within a minute, the dragon faded, lightning momentarily playing around her body, shot through with red streaks of fire. She met Branok's gaze, ignoring the minor pain that had accompanied the arrival of the dragon. It had been nothing compared to what she'd experienced before. "Are you satisfied?"

Branok gestured towards the bottles of wine. "These will work?"

Meikah nodded. Once more she knew the spell and how it functioned after having read it a single time. "They'll remove all spells on each person it's used on. The good and the bad spells. It can't tell the difference between them."

"Thank you," Branok said.

Again she nodded, somehow finding the courage to speak the thoughts that had been bothering her since talking to Naya. "You should consider making changes in the law about how necromancers are treated. Like you did when it comes to dragons."

"Dragons aren't evil," Branok said. "Not like necromancers. Even you must agree they are since your dragon is protecting you from necromancer spells."

"Do you think I'm evil?" Meikah asked.

"You will be if you do more spells than your dragon can protect you against. It can't be helped. Necromancy corrupts the mind and warps your sense of what's right and wrong." Branok gestured towards the bottles of wine. "One spell too many and you will be evil."

"Not every necromancer is evil," Kellan said. "Some can use their abilities without being corrupted by them."

Branok met his gaze. "They are so rare they might not exist."

Kellan continued to meet the King's gaze, his voice firm. "But they do exist."

"The laws won't be changed," Branok stated.

Chapter Twenty-Nine

Meikah was surprised at how disappointed she was at hearing Branok's words. She'd known it would make very little difference telling him, but obviously she'd hoped anyway. "Thank you for seeing us."

Branok nodded. "Thank you for your service to my country."

"Does this mean you're once more in Meikah's debt since she prevented your prison from being broken into and the necros set free?" Kellan asked.

Branok studied Kellan for a moment before inclining his head and turning to Meikah. "You won't always be able to collect on one favour only to replace it with another."

"I understand," Meikah said.

"I'll have someone show you out." Branok summoned a servant who led them through the castle.

Meikah was glad to be walking away from the castle. She turned to Daveth. "Why doesn't my dragon always protect me as well as yours does?"

"You need to train it so it'll protect you against all levels of danger. From the minor all the way to the major. In the beginning, it's only the worst of dangers it protects you from," Daveth said.

"Even without training, its ability to protect you will improve," Marta assured her.

"It'll improve better with training." Daveth studied Meikah. "We should start your training as soon as possible."

Meikah shrugged. As much as she wanted to accept his offer, there were other things they needed to worry about first. Such as Naya's offer. And what Tolmerr would do about them disobeying him. She turned to Kellan. "Do we have to see Tolmerr now?"

Kellan chuckled. "We could say we didn't want to disturb him after how long we were with the King. That we thought he'd probably be asleep since it's the early hours of the morning."

"It might be best to leave now so he can't take us to task for disobeying him," Shade suggested. "Especially if we plan to go after the rest of the necromancers."

"What about my grandparents?" Meikah asked.

"We can't leave them here," Kellan said. "We want Tolmerr to think we've headed for home. That way he'll notify Danton we need to be punished for insubordination and completely leave it up to him as to how it's done." Kellan grinned. "You can bet he won't be throwing us out of the Assassins Of The Dead."

"If we can't leave my grandparents here, what can we do with them?" Meikah asked. "We can't exactly take them to Naya with us."

"I know of a farmhouse we can stay in," Shade said. "At least until we figure out where Naya takes you and discover somewhere closer to stay. The farmers offered me a room to stay if I could help them clear the overgrowth from one of their far paddocks. I can set it on fire and use the wind to send the flames in the direction they need to go."

Meikah stopped and faced Shade, sending an apologetic glance at the person walking past that they stopped in front of. "Accepting Naya's offer will be dangerous."

Shade smiled. "When isn't being an assassin dangerous-?"

Meikah laughed softly. "I suppose." She looked at each of her companions. Marta nodded, as did Daveth, and Kellan grinned. Again she laughed, a touch of wryness to it. "I guess I'm in." She couldn't exactly say no when they were all wanting to go after the rest of them. Not when it hinged on her accepting Naya's offer. She glanced over her shoulder in the direction of Garven's home. "What will we do if there's another messenger waiting for us?"

Kellan grinned. "Distract him. But I highly doubt Tolmerr will send another. Not while he believes we're with the King. We'll leave a letter behind for him. I'll ask Garven to send it at daylight."

"Will he wait that long?" Meikah asked.

"Of course he will. He won't want to disturb anyone by sending it at what he'd consider an unreasonable hour." Kellan slung an arm around Shade and Meikah's shoulders, again starting towards his uncle's place. "He'll grumble a bit about being asked, but I'm sure he'll do it."

Reaching Garven's home, Meikah was able to take her grandparents aside and let them know about their plans, all the time wishing she could have crawled into bed. Staying awake was becoming an effort.

Isha shook her head once Meikah had finished informing them. "No, Meikie. It's too dangerous. Can't someone else go?"

"You heard her, love," Maksim said. "The offer was only made to her because they think she bound a dragon to her sword."

"What were you thinking using necromancer spells?" Isha demanded.

"The dragon protected me," Meikah said.

"You didn't know it would," Isha protested.

Maksim put an arm around Isha's shoulders. "Come, my love. We need to get organised. We don't want Meikah in more trouble with Tolmerr." He kept his arm around his wife as they walked towards their bedroom.

Meikah sent him a grateful smile when he glanced over his shoulder. He answered her with a wink. Her smiled turned into a grin and she turned away when she saw Isha about to check behind her. The last thing she needed was her grandmother catching her grinning at their retreating figures. She headed for the bedroom she'd been staying in and quickly packed her gear, ready at about the same time as her grandparents.

She found Kellan by the front door, handing a letter to Garven who was complaining about being woken from a sound sleep.

"What do you need me to send this off to Cryptic Ramblings for?" Garven glanced at the letter he held. "I still think you could have waited until daybreak to leave. All this rushing around is unnecessary."

"Someone at Cryptic Ramblings was expecting me to visit them later. We're not leaving unnecessarily early. Maksim has to report to the Duke regarding the matter he was sent to investigate and inform him of some other things he discovered during his mission," Kellan said.

Garven glanced at the letter he held. "It's not even addressed to anyone. Just has the name of the bookshop."

"That's all it needs," Kellan said. "It'll get to the right person."

"All this haste to leave," Garven grumbled. "Can't see how another day would have hurt. Always rushing about. Surely the Duke won't expect you to go rushing about at this hour."

"Sounds like you don't want us to go," Kellan said.

"I can't wait to see the back of you," Garven stated. "But you could cause less inconvenience during the process of leaving." He glared at Kellan. "Upsetting my household like this."

Meikah held out her hand to Garven, half surprised he actually shook it. "Thank you for letting us stay here."

"Not like I had much choice in the matter," Garven grumbled with a glance at Kellan.

He grinned at his uncle. "You know you loved having us stay. We kept your housekeeper from boring you with all her gossip."

They traipsed outside to where a wagon waited for them. Daveth helped Isha onto it, his swords now in two sheathes Shade had procured for him. Meikah climbed in the back of the wagon, waiting until they were heading down the street before she asked Shade the question that had been bothering her. "What about the carriage and men the Duke sent with us?"

"I advised them to return to him," Shade said. "That Maksim had other things to do in the area before we all return to Dreyton."

Meikah glanced skywards. "Where are we going to stay while we wait for midnight?"

"We can get settled in at the farmhouse, have a sleep, and if there's enough time, Kellan might be able to help me make a start on clearing that paddock," Shade suggested.

Meikah made herself comfortable in the back of the wagon. Yawning, she closed her eyes for a minute only to realise, when Kellan was shaking her awake, that she'd slept through the journey to the farmhouse.

"Shade has organised everything. They weren't exactly happy to be disturbed an hour before dawn, but they're pleased enough he can help them with the paddock," Kellan said.

Chapter Thirty

Meikah glanced around, her ability to see in the dark taking a few seconds to work as she struggled to push away the last shreds of sleep. They had pulled up in front of a small cabin, a larger farmhouse set off to the right and a barn well behind it. She stumbled out of the wagon and inside the cabin. It was as basic as the exterior had suggested.

Isha was setting a lit lantern on the scarred, timber table, four chairs set around it, and Shade was lighting the wood fire oven that was beside a window on the far wall. There was a single room to the left, a double bed and a bunk bed crammed into it, a timber chest between them against the wall.

Isha looked up with a smile. "The housekeeper gave me some supplies for the journey. If you give me a minute, I'll make tea and then heat something for you to eat before you have a proper sleep."

"Will you be all right here?" Meikah asked.

Isha nodded. "It's warm and dry. We'll be fine."

Maksim entered with an armful of firewood that he set beside the wood fire oven. He turned to face Meikah. "You be careful with those necromancers. Don't trust them and leave if you think things are going to go bad in a big way. Bringing them in isn't worth your life."

She was half tempted to point out that she couldn't die. Lose her body, yes, but that wouldn't bring her existence to an end. She'd still be able to interact with the world and those in it. "I'll take care."

Shade stepped away from the oven. "I'll see if Kellan wants to give me a hand with that paddock. We might as well get a bit of work done before we have a sleep. That way we'll be more rested before you meet up with Naya. Taking care of the paddock is the least we can do in exchange for somewhere to stay for a few days." He strode from the cabin, Marta, who'd been about to enter, stepping back so he could exit.

She came in, remaining by the doorway. "Daveth and I will see if there's anything we can do to help clear the paddock."

Meikah nodded, glad of the short time she'd have with her grandparents before they slept and she had to leave. Not that she knew if joining Naya to discover more of their plan and figure out a way to capture all of them was a good idea. She thought of Hincke and his plans, glad he was imprisoned. Going after them was a good idea. Especially if they felt the same way as he felt. As much as she wanted necromancers to be treated differently, at least until they succumbed to being full necromancers, Hincke's way wasn't how to go about it.

When Isha poured the tea, they sat at the table talking about general things, Meikah's mind turning to home as Isha filled Maksim in on some of the gossip from Dreyton. Thankfully, none of it was about her. She took a sip of her tea, nodding in agreement with something Isha had said. Most of her thoughts were focused on returning home. What would happen when the two dragon touched warriors faced Amiel again? Would Amiel remember them? Would he remember he was the one who'd caused their deaths? Maybe trying to take down the rest of Hincke's necromancers wasn't such a bad task after all.

When Kellan, Shade, Marta and Daveth came in, Isha served food, once more asking Meikah if she was certain they needed to accept Naya's offer so they could infiltrate the necromancers. Meikah only smiled, glad she'd taken a bite and her mouth was full.

They slept the rest of the day, not waking until late in the evening. Isha prepared food while they prepared to leave, only having an hour before they had to go. She took the plate off Meikah when she rose from the table, finished eating.

"Leave it, Meikie. I'll take care of it once you're gone." She set the plate back on the table. "You'd best be on your way if you mean to do this."

Meikah hugged her grandmother. "I'll be back before you know it."

Isha's arms tightened around Meikah. "I wish I could believe that." She followed them to the front door, where she stood with her arm around Maksim's waist and his around her shoulders.

Meikah mounted the horse Maksim had saddled for her and gave her grandparents a last wave before she kept her gaze on the road ahead. She couldn't help thinking about everything that had occurred since they'd come to the capital. They'd done more than they'd expected. Now she didn't know where they'd end up.

Shade, who'd been riding alongside them, disappeared amongst the trees while Marta and Daveth returned to the dagger and sword at Meikah's sides, Marta having returned the dagger during their meal. Meikah wanted to protest. It didn't feel safe with only the two of them riding along the road. Not that where they were heading was even slightly safe.

She remained silent as they continued towards their destination. As they approached, she saw a spirit standing in the middle of the road, watching them. He reminded her of all the ones from Durnning Island. What had happen to them when the necromancers were given the wine? It hadn't occurred to her, when's Shade had suggested the spell, that it would sever their ties to the necromancers. But it seemed like the most likely outcome. She couldn't think about it right now. Not while she was walking into danger.

"Who do you await a message from?" the spirit asked once they were close enough.

Meikah stopped her horse in front of him. He wore clothes that were about a century out of date. "Naya."

The spirit bowed deeply and stepped to the side, gesturing along the road. "Travel that way until you come to a narrow road to the right. It will eventually come to a fork. Take the left one." He bowed again. "Safe travels, young lady." He turned to Kellan. "And to you also, young man."

"Thank you." Meikah urged her horse forward, repeating the directions over and over in her mind. The road was silent, the trees pressing in on each side of them. She wished she could speak to Kellan and ask him what he was thinking about their plans. But she didn't know if they were being watched by someone other than Shade. It made sense that they'd be watched. Particularly since Naya hadn't seemed the trusting sort. Nor had Ervass.

Half a mile after turning down the left fork in the narrow, dirt road, Naya rode out from amongst the trees, stopping in the middle of the road twenty feet ahead of them to wait for them to approach. "Do I take it you're interested in a better life?"

Before Meikah could answer, Kellan spoke. "How do we know there are enough of you to make a difference? That the King's soldiers didn't capture most of your organisation."

"We only sent a third of our people to that clearing with Hincke. If all had gone with him, we would have won," Naya said. "We won't make that mistake again." She turned to Meikah. "Now what is your answer? Do you want a better life than the one you can have under the current laws?"

"I'm interested in necromancers being treated better," Meikah said truthfully.

Naya smiled, this one nowhere near as frightening as her other one. "Then you've made the right choice joining us." Her smile vanished and her eyes narrowed. "But be warned. If you do wrong by us, we will make you pay. We'll also be watching you carefully until you prove yourselves." Her gaze flickered from Meikah to Kellan, then back again. "Understand?"

Meikah nodded, speaking when it looked like Naya expected it. "I understand." She glanced at Kellan.

He also nodded. "I wouldn't have expected anything less." He grinned. "Now where are we headed? It's been a long day and I'm looking forward to crawling into bed."

Naya gave him a look of disgust. "You'll soon learn that rest has to be earned, like every other privilege." She turned to Meikah, studying her.

Meikah was tempted to ask if there was something wrong. She remained silent instead, glad that they'd had plenty of sleep.

Naya smiled again, causing a shiver to run down Meikah's spine. "Welcome to the necromancer resistance.

One day, this country will be ours." She turned her horse to face the direction Meikah and Kellan had been travelling in, glancing over her shoulder. "Come along then."

Meikah followed Naya, Kellan remaining at her side. If the necromancer resistance took over, the entire country would be in danger. Including her family. She wasn't about to let that happen. The image of Naya's smile remained in her mind, along with the thought of how large the organisation was. Naya would enjoy killing all who stood in her way and would use whatever power and means it took to achieve her goals. Again Meikah shivered. It was going to take more than a plan to stop the resistance. It was likely to take a miracle. And she wasn't certain either of them could come up with one.

Free Ebook

Subscribe to Avril's newsletter and receive a free ebook. This ebook is exclusive to those on her mailing list. To find out more about this offer visit:

https://www.avrilsabine.com/free-ebook

*

We value your privacy and will not sell, rent, exchange or loan your email address to third parties. Your information is confidential and you are under no obligation to remain on the mailing list and can unsubscribe at any time.

Acknowledgements

As always, thank you to my usual crew. I appreciate your help.

To The Reader

If you enjoyed this book, why not consider leaving a review to help other readers discover it too? Reader engagement is one of the few ways that lets an author know readers want more books in a particular series or genre. So leave a review and tell friends, not only about this book but also about other ones you've enjoyed, so you can continue to enjoy books by your favourite authors for years to come.

Dreams are meant to be lived,
Avril.

About The Author

Avril is an Australian author who lives with her family on acreage in South East Queensland. She writes mostly young adult and children's speculative fiction, but has been known to dabble in other genres. You can find more information about her at https://www.avrilsabine.com where you can also subscribe to her newsletter to be kept informed about new releases, current projects, blog posts and exclusive news.

Titles By Avril Sabine

Stories about strong characters and characters who discover their strengths.

Series

Assassins Of The Dead– Young Adult Fantasy /Paranormal

Book 1: Dark Blade

Book 2: Dragon Touched

Book 3: Society Against Vampires

Book 4: King's Request

Book 5: Duke's Courier

Dragon Blood– Young Adult Urban Fantasy (with elements of romance)

(5 book series)

Book 1: Pliethin

Book 2: Wyvern

Book 3: Surety

Book 4: Knight

Book 5: Mage

Dragon Mage- Young Adult Urban Fantasy (with elements of romance)

(Series two of Dragon Blood series)

Book 1: Promise

Dragon Blood Chronicles- Young Adult Urban Fantasy (with elements of romance)

(Companion stand alone series to Dragon Blood)

Book 1: Oath

Book 2: Betrayed

Guardians Of The Round Table- Young Adult Fantasy LitRPG

(Co-written with Storm and Rhys Petersen)

Book 1: Dexterity Fail

Book 2: Goblin Boots

Book 3: Singed Feathers

Book 4: Frog Mage

Book 5: Crystal Mine

Book 6: Cursed Harp

Book 7: Treasure Seeker

Rosie's Rangers- Young Adult Western Steampunk

(6 book series)

Book 1: Justice

Book 2: Vengeance

Book 3: Treachery

Book 4: Accused

Book 5: Wanted

Book 6: Corruption

Mark Of Kings- Children's Fantasy

(Upper middle grade/preteen)

(4 book series)

Book 1: The Arena

Book 2: The Island

Book 3: The Assassin

Book 4: The King

Stand Alone Series

Demon Hunters- Young Adult Urban Fantasy/Horror (with elements of romance)
Book 1: Blood Sacrifice

Book 2: Retribution

Book 3: Tainted

Book 4: Premonition

Book 5: Cursed

Book 6: Feud

Book 7: Extrication

Plea Of The Damned- Young Adult Urban Fantasy/Paranormal
(6 book series)

Book 1: Forgive Me Lucy

Book 2: Forgive Me Aiden

Book 3: Forgive Me Jena

Book 4: Forgive Me Kobe

Book 5: Forgive Me Marti

Book 6: Forgive Me Dawson

Realms Of The Fae- Young Adult Urban Fantasy (with elements of romance)

The Sword (short story in Like A Girl Anthology)
Call Forth The Wild Hunt (Short story in Summer Solstice Shenanigans Anthology)
Heart Of Stone
Book 1: A Debt Owed
Book 2: Marked By The Hunt
Book 3: The Magic Collector
Book 4: An Unexpected Betrayal
Book 5: Imprisoned By Iron
Book 6: Woven From Dreams

Fairytales Retold (Short Stories)

Snow-White And Rose-Red
The Twelve Brothers
The Light Princess
Beauty And The Beast
Sleeping Beauty
Aschenputtel
The Golden Bird
The Frog Prince

The Death Of Koshchei The Deathless

Myths And Legends Retold (Short Stories)

Ion, Son Of Apollo
Sir Gawain And The Maid With The Narrow Sleeves
Princess Ilse, The Giant's Daughter

Young Adult Novels

Young Adult Fantasy (with elements of romance)

Elf Sight
Earth Bound

Young Adult Urban Fantasy

Stone Warrior (with elements of romance)
The Jungle Inside

Young Adult Contemporary (with elements of romance)

Through Your Eyes
The Ugly Stepsister
Perfect Little Princess

Young Adult Contemporary/Paranormal

Whispers In The Dark (with elements of romance and
same sex relationships)
Over Too Soon (with elements of romance)

Young Adult Sci-Fi

Experiment X-One-Six (Urban Sci-Fi/Superheroes)
An Endless Dawn (Post Apocalyptic Sci-Fi)

Children's Books

Dragon Lord (Preteen/early teens) (Fantasy)
The Irish Wizard (Upper middle grade) (Urban Fanta-sy)

Short Stories

Urban Fantasy

Eternally Late
Dealings With Joe
Glimpses (short story in That Moment When Anthology)

Contemporary

The Brat Next Door

Fantasy LitRPG

(Set in the same world as Guardians Of The Round Table Series)
Tales Of Inadon 1: The Disc (Co-written with Storm and Rhys Petersen) (short story in Game On! Anthology)

Post Apocalyptic Sci-Fi

Compulsive Directive

Nonfiction

A Year Of Weekly Writing Exercises (Creative Writing)
Cooking For Families With Allergies (Cooking) (Co-written with Storm Petersen)
Tell Me A Story, Grandma (Memoir)

Online Course

Overview Of Independently Publishing A Book

For the most up to date details on available titles visit:

www.avrilsabine.com/books/bibliography

Assassins Of The Dead Series

To learn more about this series visit:

www.avrilsabine.com/series/aotd

BOOKS AVAILABLE IN THE ASSASSINS OF THE DEAD SERIES

Book 1: Dark Blade

Book 2: Dragon Touched

Book 3: Society Against Vampires

Book 4: King's Request

Book 5: Duke's Courier

Disclaimer

This is a work of fiction. Names, characters, businesses, places, events and incidents are either the products of the author's imagination or used in a fictitious manner. Any resemblance to actual persons, living or dead, or actual events is purely coincidental. The opinions expressed or beliefs held are those of the characters and should not be assumed to be the opinions or beliefs of the author.

www.ingramcontent.com/pod-product-compliance
Lightning Source LLC
Chambersburg PA
CBHW020758190726
48285CB00006B/2094